SLEEP ROUGH TONIGHT

SLEEP ROUGH

DUTTON BOOKS   BOOKS   NEW YORK

TONIGHT

IAN BONE

The poem on page 211 is taken from a gravestone in Myponga Cemetery, South Australia. The child's real name and age have not been used.

Library of Congress Cataloging-in-Publication Data
Bone, Ian, date.
Sleep rough tonight / by Ian Bone.—1st American ed.
p.   cm.
Summary: Teased and bullied by his high-school classmates,
Alex Pimentino tries to prove his worth by following the commands of a former student just released from prison, but finds that his real strength comes from doing the right thing.
ISBN 0-525-47373-4
[1. Bullying—Fiction. 2. Stalking—Fiction. 3. Conduct of life—Fiction. 4. High schools—Fiction.
5. Schools—Fiction. 6. Friendship—Fiction. 7. Self-perception—Fiction.] I. Title.
PZ7.B63697Sl   2005
[Fic]—dc22   2004052714

Published in the United States 2005 by Dutton Books,
a member of Penguin Group (USA) Inc.
345 Hudson Street, New York, New York 10014
www.penguin.com/youngreaders

First published in 2004 by Penguin Books Australia,
250 Camberwell Road, Camberwell, Victoria 3124, Australia

Typography by Heather Wood
Printed in USA / First American Edition

TO THE BONE MEN

*My grandfather, Peter, whose battlefield was bush politics;
his son, Max, a farm boy who went to live in the city;
his son, Ian, who always wants to know more;
his son, Jack, who can reach to the top of the world.*

SLEEP ROUGH TONIGHT

THE JOCKEY

IT TAKES A WHOLE VILLAGE TO RAISE A CHILD.

—AFRICAN PROVERB

CHAPTER ONE

He was back in the boys' room again. Dragged into the red-brick building by a giant with acne and peach fuzz. Another dunking. Alex didn't ask for mercy, nor did he cry out. Instead he talked, working his way into Barry Pilsener's ear like an annoying flea, buzzing and biting with each word.

"I don't want to complain or nothing," said Alex, his feet sometimes running, sometimes scraping along the ground. "But you totally suck as a toilet-dunker, Barry."

Unfortunately, his tormentor couldn't hear him. A noisy crush of boys had filled the bathroom, each yelling for blood. Alex's voice, muffled as it was under the boy's humongous armpit, was lost in the din. It was not much more than a vibration against the giant's rib cage, but still it would not stop. Not for lack of audience, not for physical pain, and not for fear of reprisal.

Alex twisted his head around into a painful angle so that he could see his surroundings. Brief snatches flashed before his eyes like photographs. A row of steel faucets, insolent soldiers lined up for the execution. Beneath them the chrome sink, scratched and dented from flying legs. Behind, the redbrick walls, covered in messages from long-ago students.

"You, like, totally screwed it up last time," said Alex, swallowing fuzz from Barry's sweater.

His tormentor paused before an open stall, and the gathering pack cheered. Would this be the ultimate moment? Ear-piercing whistles cracked the air as Barry's brain slowly ticked over. Tick. Tock. Nothing seemed to be surfacing.

From his angle, Alex could see the boy's leg stretching all the way to the ground, his school pants bending like a wild slide to the scuffed shoe below. He was distracted for a brief moment, removed from the drama and the adrenaline. Alex could feel the pain in his ears and neck, could hear the tiny voice in his mind questioning what the hell he was doing here. He shut them out. This was the game. The toilet, Pilsener's indecision, the cheering pack of boys behind him.

This was the game that had started the way it always did—with a lonely boy roaming the school wastelands all lunchtime. With Alex, that annoying kid who walked from football game to gossip corner to senior area and back again, bouncing like the shiny silver orb in a pinball machine. Bing! Ding! Off the group of girls near the cafeteria, who looked down at him with a sneer. Past the small groups and the lone kids and the slow sandwich eaters.

Into the middle school yard he landed, where the "Bald Eagle" patrolled, hands behind his back, gray cardigan slightly askew. Mimicking the teacher's movements behind him, getting a laugh until the Eagle turned with a, "Hi, ho, what's this, then?" And Alex, standing restlessly, watched the teacher's bushy eyebrows stick out like awnings. "Mr. Pimentino, isn't it?" said the Eagle, his nasally voice wrapping itself around his sarcasm. "Nothing better to do than bother hardworking, selfless teachers? Isn't there somebody in this school with the patience to be your friend?"

The lonely boy responds with smiles, all smiles, holding his hands behind his back, his disrespectful middle finger tall and straight. Then running, hearing one of the junior girls telling the Eagle, "He was doing that finger thing to you, sir."

Gone.

From one edge to another, until he finally rolled into the seniors' area. It had been a few days since his last encounter with them, a memory that was obviously fresher in Alex's mind than theirs. They ignored his presence, arranged as they were on the bench against the wall. Some sitting on the top of the backrest slats, others standing with hands in pockets, long, strong legs perched up against the seat. He stood watching them. How assured they looked. How tall. There was a confident air about them, a stillness that was crying out to be challenged.

Then one of the seniors glanced in his direction, and Alex called out, "How ya doing?" The senior blinked in slow motion, turning back to his group. Alex could see a subtle change come over them. A shoulder thrown forward more than the usual, a neck tighter than it had been, a sly joke that produced too loud a response.

They knew he was there.

This was the game, watching them, waiting for an opening. Nodding his head whenever one was incautious enough to make eye contact. Standing with his hands in his pockets, his heart racing, wondering when to make his move. He could hear noises around him, kids shouting across at mates, voices raised in dispute, a metal basket knocked sideways.

Alex sniffed. Threw his head back.

Then Barry Pilsener turned slowly, and for a second, it seemed that the sun might have been blotted out. He was straight to the point.

"Piss off."

"Whatcha up to, Barry?" Alex asked. "Getting any?"

"Getting a pain from you."

"Hey, that's not bad," said Alex, a hint of genuine appreciation in his voice. He took a step closer, his mouth tingling with an acrid taste, his legs twitching with a life of their own.

It was courage of a sort.

Or stupidity.

"Piss off," repeated Barry, then he turned his back on him again.

Alex waited, but the seniors had suddenly lost interest in him, certain that they'd dealt with the nuisance. He was gone. Gone.

Now he would make his play.

Taking another step closer, Alex thrust his hands deeper into his pockets and opened his mouth, knowing full well that a single sound would bring their fury down on him. Knowing that they'd given him his chance.

"Hey, Barry," he yelled. "You gotta love me, don't ya?"

And he was back here in the boys' room again.

Leering faces grinned at the spectacle before them, their shouts echoing around the bathroom. Elbows flew carelessly, knocking scruffy heads. Boys in the front row were jostled and shoved for their vantage point.

"I don't like to criticize you, Barry," said Alex, head squeezed, sweater twisted, "but I just know you're gonna make a mess of this dunking again. . . ."

The crowd seemed fairly confident in the giant's ability. They stood before the stalls while doors were flung open, revealing tanks and toilet bowls and unspeakable smudges on the floor. Barry moved along the row of doors, scraping Alex's knee, and the mob followed.

"I bet you don't even get me wet," shouted Alex over the din.

Still no response from his tormentor. What was the point of humor if it was lost in the noise? Alex twisted his head around as far as he could without tearing his neck muscles and tried again.

"The trouble is, you're too stupid."

At last, he had an audience. This comment earned him a painful tap on the top of his head from the giant's knuckles. The crowd cheered. As mangled as he was in the boy's grip, Alex was encouraged by the noise of the mob. He was the proverbial moth, and the smell of burning wings was all too present in his nostrils.

"In fact," continued Alex, "you're so stupid, the last time you blew your nose, your brains came out."

Barry responded with a quick crush on Alex's throat.

"You're so stupid, you think a toilet is a place to get a quick drink."

He was pushed into a door frame and leaned on by Barry's considerable weight. The mob started yelling. Surely the kid would ask for mercy.

"Now me . . . ," said Alex, but he couldn't continue. He waited for his breath to return. At last Barry leaned back, and Alex gulped in air before he was dragged onward again. With his voice thin and cracking, he continued. "Me, I happen to be an expert in toilet-dunking. . . ."

Which was probably true, although Barry knew quite a bit about it as well. Dunking was a shared experience, one that would *not* wind up on their résumés. Barry paused in front of the last stall, his chest heaving from the effort of dragging the little comedian to the bowl. Alex's head bobbed up and down with every breath, making him look like a deranged puppet.

"You ever actually used a toilet before, Barry?" he asked. "Or do you squat over a hole?"

"Shut up."

The giant barged into the last stall, ramming Alex's shoulder against the door frame on the way in. He flung the boy onto the floor and barked, "Kneel down there!"

"I don't mean to criticize or anything . . . ," Alex began.

"Kneel down!"

A kick in the back of his legs, a bruiser. Alex knelt on the floor. "Kneeling won't actually work. . . . It's all the wrong angle . . ."

Barry grabbed him by the collar and rammed his head toward the toilet. A sharp pain stung Alex's lip where he accidentally bit it, and the salty taste of blood filled his mouth.

"This'll teach you," shouted Barry, shoving Alex's face roughly into the toilet bowl.

"Teach me for what?" shouted Alex, his words echoing comically around the bowl.

Barry paused, perhaps to remember Alex's supposed crime, or perhaps to rethink his dunking technique. Alex leaped into the pause. "For tying my shoelaces this morning?" he suggested. "For waking up, for wearing my school uniform? . . ."

"For being an annoying little scumbag," yelled Barry, pushing Alex's face further into the bowl so that his head disappeared. A roar erupted from behind. The news was reported, the deed had been done. Satisfied with this half attempt at a dunking, Barry released his grip with a brutal flick that caused Alex's ears to bang violently against the ceramic bowl.

The crowd departed, but Alex stayed there for a second or two, listening as they dispersed. Stayed until it was relatively quiet, then removed his head from the foul bowl and stood painfully, the bruise on the back of his thigh already throbbing. Straightening his clothing, Alex walked over to the sink. He stood on tiptoes to get a quick look at himself in the mirror. His reflection showed a wet forehead and a few strands of damp hair hanging loosely on his face. Hardly the dunking that Barry Pilsener had been hoping for.

The swelling was already evident on his lip, and Alex played his tongue over the wound, enjoying the tangy taste. He had a cheeky face, covered in a fine spray of freckles, which made him look wicked even when he wasn't trying to be. Alex pulled on the wet strands of hair that hung loosely over his forehead. He twirled them into a knife shape, and it stood rigid from his blond fringe for a moment, then flopped down again. Washing himself with the liquid pink soap, Alex dried his face and hair in the hand dryer. Even though he was short, he had to squat low to receive the warm air. The effort made him feel nauseous after awhile, so he stood, leaning against the wall.

He combed his hair with his fingers, recalling the vivid images of the dunking. He saw every detail. Grinning faces. Wild cheers.

Excited laughter. Screaming idiots. Boys. Bullies. Peers. Captains. He knew each and every one. Then another image came to him. Another face in the crowd. Alex froze.

His head swayed slightly.

His lip throbbed.

The Jockey. Was he really there? It must have been a mistake. A crazy vision. Or maybe it was a kid who just looked like him. The Jockey couldn't possibly have been there. Alex tried to think. The Jockey had been locked up behind bars all last year, then they'd let him out. But the story was he'd gone to live in Queensland with his mom. A long, safe distance away.

Could he possibly be back?

Dancing on his toes, Alex tried to shake off the horrible question. Stay sharp, stay alert. Look up, up, up, he told himself. No fear. He took a long, deep drink from the only working faucet, then banged his fist on the surface of the sink, making a deep, echoing drumming. It soothed him, rocked his bones with its growling voice. *Boom! Boom!* Time to move. Time to move! Smile now. Be happy. With a final grin at his reflection, Alex burst out of the bathroom and yelled, "Here I am!"

The area was virtually empty, no sign of the mob. They were back at their seats in the adjacent school yard. He'd been too slow. Should he go over to them and parade his dry head? A casual stroll past? A long, pointed walk?

He heard a foot scraping on the ground.

And turned.

Near the bike rack, leaning against the chain-link fence with a half smile on his lips . . . So, it really *was* him.

"Oh," said Alex, looking down at his feet instinctively.

The Jockey smiled, then said, "Alex Pimentino." It wasn't so much a greeting or a question as a simple statement of fact.

"Gotta go," said Alex, and he walked away as quickly as he could without running.

The Jockey stared hard at the departing boy, then shook his head slowly before walking in the opposite direction. Alex did not look back. All he could feel was the tight wrenching of his throat and the pain in his legs as he struggled to stay calm.

For the first time that day, he felt truly frightened.

CHAPTER TWO

"**W**hat would happen if the hunter farted?"

It seemed like a fair enough question, but Mrs. Fulton didn't see it that way. Alex scored the usual laugh for it, the sudden impact of the word and the concept shaking some of his classmates out of their boredom. A few of the front-row dwellers rolled their eyes, but he never saw them, perched as he was in the middle, right in the line of Mrs. F's fire.

Alex glared back at her. Why was it always his fault? Blame it on someone else this time. Blame it on his classmates who allowed the questions to dry up. Blame it on the story they'd just heard, or blame it on the storyteller. Hadn't the guy just spent the last twenty minutes prancing about on the auditorium stage, eyes afire, muscles rippling under the sheen of his fine black skin as he told the tale of the hunter and the lion? Hadn't he made them think about such questions?

Not that Alex had actually been all that interested in the guy's story at first. He'd shuffled into the auditorium like everyone else to sit low in his chair, out of the teacher's eyeline, out of sight. Once settled, he swirled down a troubled and twisted road into his thoughts, trying to figure out how the Jockey could have returned like that. Why did they even let him back? And why had no one told him about it?

But, of course, no one *would* tell him about it. He was nobody, wasn't he?

As he'd sat grinding these questions around in his head, the storyteller's voice had been nothing more than a drone in the background, rising and falling. Then a word or two broke through, a phrase that seemed to mock him. Alex sat up a little, watching the storyteller over a row of his classmates' heads.

"Kamau's knees knock with fear. His mouth tastes like a rhinoceros's underbelly," boomed the actor.

He was creeping up on an imaginary sleeping lion, quivering with a palpable fear. Alex almost felt sorry for the guy. This style of storytelling went out in primary school. It was a pity that no one had bothered to tell Mrs. Fulton that. The whole performance was part of her course, a study of African village life. The men, the women, the religions, the food they ate, and the strange things they made their boys go out and do. Like steal a piece from a lion's mane to prove that they're a man.

The storyteller patrolled the middle of the stage, casting his gaze around the audience. His words built a picture, his body sculpted an imaginary scene with the language of hands, eyes, and torso.

For a moment, Alex was drawn in, then his worried mind took over.

And the memories flooded back.

"How's it going, little bro?" That was the Jockey, smiling at him so long ago, knocking him on the shoulder, gripping him playfully around the neck. "You're a cool kid, eh?" He *was* a cool kid, then. The Jockey would single him out, treat him as a mate, an equal, then depart, leaving behind the impact of his presence. It would stay for days, that wide sea that he created.

Alex remembered . . .

"Run!"

A shout from the stage crashed him back to the present, and he saw the actor running to hide behind a "tree."

"Oh, how Kamau's knees knock," shouted the actor. "How his toes curl. That lion is supposed to be asleep. Kamau's brothers are all hiding up a tree. 'Don't be such a chicken,' they whisper. 'The lion is only dreaming. Go to it, we're right behind you. . . .' So poor Kamau leaves the safety of his tree."

The storyteller crept forward, painfully slow, alone on the stage, arms held cautiously before him. He was vulnerable to attack, looking left, right, his dreadlocked hair flapping with each movement. The man was a story in himself.

"Still Kamau waits," he said, eyes all wide-whites and frightened pupils. "His brothers call to him, 'Kamau, hurry. That old lion will die of boredom before you get to him!' Kamau feels the power drain from his body with the terror, tastes the puke in his mouth. This is a lion before him, a very crafty lion . . ."

And Alex remembered.

A disturbance in the shopping center parking lot, a few years back. Watching over the road as a ring of boys shouted, pushed, then parted to allow the Jockey out, a wild look in his eyes. And still Alex watched as the crowd scattered and a broken boy was left behind, face aching, body hurt.

"A lion is dangerous and sly," the storyteller warned. "And

Lisimba is the most cunning of them all . . . a fierce old warrior who has tasted warm blood many times before. Can he really be asleep?"

Thoughts crept into Alex's mind, of that night outside his father's store when everything had changed. Of that one moment that had ruined it all. Of the Jockey in prison.

"Take care!" The actor's shout startled him. "A lion will slice you into pieces then toss you into a salad before you have a chance to call for your mommy. A lion will pee all over your bones for the pleasure of it." The storyteller stomped his feet loudly, looked up at the lights. "Kamau does not want to be a chicken, so he holds his arms high and asks for guidance from the ancient ancestors of his tribe. The old, dead hunters who are remembered in their tales. 'Ancestors!' he yells. 'I am sorry to disturb your well-earned rest, but how am I supposed to steal from a lion?'"

Alex could feel his throat tighten, his mind going back to the Jockey outside the bathroom. He replayed every tiny detail. Had the Jockey been angry? Threatening? He wished he'd stayed longer, waited for the Jockey to say more than just his name. Now he had nothing. Twelve months they locked him away in the Barlow Road Juvenile Detention Center. That's a long time to think, to figure out what you might say to your little "bro."

"Kamau hears thunder rolling, then Lutalo the warrior speaks to him from the clouds, saying, 'Kamau, you fool. Go upwind so the lion will not smell you.' Kamau sniffs under his arms . . . and Phew! Lutalo is right. So he walks upwind."

A long time to frame a question in your head . . .

"Sentwali the courageous one speaks to Kamau. 'Are you a spineless chicken? A giggling maiden? Think, boy! What is the only creature that will defeat a lion? That is what you must become.' Kamau shakes his head. This is no time for riddles . . ."

Alex wanted to stand, leave the auditorium, but he was hemmed in on every side by hard, sweating bodies. A tremendous restlessness took him over and he concentrated on a couple of boys in front of him for distraction. They were jabbing pens into each other. Sharp, rapid attacks. Retaliation. Hurt and be hurt. Revenge.

What had the Jockey meant by only saying his name? Just "Alex Pimentino," nothing more.

Then the actor shouted from the stage, and Alex clenched his fists, looking up to see that he'd missed the climax of the story. The storyteller was holding an imaginary piece of lion's mane in his hand, a look of triumph on his face.

The fight was over.

That was when the storyteller had sat on the edge of the stage for questions. Normally Alex would not step into the silence, but this time he really wanted to know. What *would* have happened if the hunter farted? Upwind or not, the sound would have woken that lion, then *Wham!* Did the hunter think of that when he stood in the savannah, heart racing, mouth dry?

The storyteller smiled at the question, and probably would have answered, but the bell sounded, and the pack stood, eager to go. Alex stood, too, the urge to get out stronger than the need for an answer. Then Mrs. Fulton collared him.

"I've just about had enough of you this term!" she exploded. "You are rude, offensive, annoying, and disruptive! Get to the office right away!"

Alex glared at her. The office? Again? What was her problem? All term she raved on about boring stuff that made his head go numb, and the one day she arranges something halfway interesting, he gets into trouble for asking a simple question. He refused to move.

"Now," said Mrs. Fulton quietly.

Some of the shuffling escapees paused to watch the spectacle. Alex saw the storyteller out of the corner of his eye. The guy looked embarrassed. Mrs. Fulton stood waiting, watching. Alex grabbed his school bag and stormed out of the auditorium, heading straight for the yard. Why bother with the office? It was the end of the day, anyway.

The final bell rang as he headed for the gate, the most beautiful sound of the day. Alex landed at the south bus stop, bag between his feet, a trick he'd quickly learned at Marble Hill. Bags had a habit of being whisked away and thrown over fences. He could hear the mob emerging from the school, heading his way, and he looked around nervously.

Some seniors took up positions behind him, whispering to one another. He jumped at their raucous shouts. Did the Jockey catch a bus? Would it be this one? The school public address system crackled into life, Mr. Somerville's cheerful voice squeaking through the airwaves.

". . . thank you to all the student body for yet another trouble-free day at Marble Hill High School . . ."

A loud burst of laughter erupted from behind, and Alex shuddered.

"Hey, Grub," called one of the seniors.

Alex turned around. A pimply man-boy with red hair was grinning at him, some kind of horrible suggestion in his expression.

". . . for a special smile . . ." the principal's voice continued in the background. "Suzie Jacka receives a Harmony Award . . ."

"Whatya want?" said Alex. "Did you forget the way home? Do you want me to phone your mommy for you?"

The senior shook his head. "I wouldn't be so disrespectful if I was you," he said. "Haven't you heard? Darren is back . . ."

There was a moment of silence, and the principal's amplified voice drifted across to them on the wind. ". . . so make sure you follow Jenna's example and pick up some stray trash on your way home. . . ."

Alex stared at the senior and almost smiled. What an idiot this guy was. Using the Jockey's real name.

"He's a hard man, this Darren," added the senior. "So why don't you give *him* some tips on dunking . . . ?"

The group of seniors stared at Alex, waiting for a reply. A thousand retorts sprung into his head, all designed to annoy, to sting. But then a loud hiss of bus brakes erupted behind, and Alex jumped, turning quickly to hide his embarrassment. He was startled by the noise, that was all. Just the noise.

The older boys laughed at him, then pushed past to get onto the South bus. Alex waited. He knew the rules. The seniors climbed on first, then the rest fought it out. Of course he'd challenged the rules in his early days at Marble Hill. Jumped onto the bus ahead of the rest, smiling cheekily at them, saying he had "special permission" from the principal. They took him, and his bag, off the bus unceremoniously.

Once the pack of comedians had all piled in, Alex climbed on last, nodding to the bus driver who ignored him. It was standing room only inside, kids packing the aisles, leaning over to talk to friends who'd scored a seat. Alex peered through the bodies to see one spare seat up near the back, next to a quiet girl who clutched her bag in front of her, as if for protection. She had a flushed rosy complexion and long black hair, which she wore tied back into a severe ponytail. Alex weaved his way through the crowd and sat down, shooting the girl a quick glance.

The bus moved off with a lurch, and a mob of older boys near them let out a roar. There was a restless mood in the air. The girl looked down at her feet, then she jerked forward suddenly, yelling, "Stop it!"

Two boys behind her started laughing loudly, and Alex tensed. The girl reached for her ponytail and yanked a metal clip from it, ripping several strands of hair out in the process. One of the boys leaned forward and said, "Give us back my clip."

"No," said the girl, not turning around.

"Give it back."

She threw the clip into the aisle of the bus and it bounced off someone's butt before landing in among the crush of feet. The owner of the butt didn't feel a thing. The owner of the clip pushed his fist between Alex and the girl. There it was, this curled-up hand that looked as if it had once held something.

"Did you drop your ice cream, mate?" said Alex, trying to break the tension.

"Shut up, Grub," said the owner of the clip. He glared at the girl, saying, "You're a stupid, ugly idiot."

"And you're a moron," replied the girl.

"Even your hair is ugly," retorted the boy.

"Even your friends are morons," said the girl.

There was a pause as the older boy took in the latest retort. How would he reply? With more words? Or something else? Alex turned in his seat, and the girl looked at him, a hint of pleading in her eyes. Eventually the clip owner withdrew his fist and muttered something to his friend, who laughed. All was quiet.

When at last the bus arrived at Alex's stop, he let out a small sigh of relief, then stood slowly. The girl stirred next to him. Alex weaved his way down the aisle, which had partially cleared of bodies by now. He could see the clip lying on the floor, so he kicked it casually under one of the seats. Giving the bus driver a wave (and knowing it would be ignored), Alex jumped from the top step of the bus onto the footpath and beat a hasty retreat toward home. It was a twenty-yard walk along the main road to his street, which he turned into at great speed. Then he stopped and waited.

After a few moments, the girl from the bus came around the corner and smiled at him.

"Hey," she said.

"Hey, Marta," he replied, smiling back. Then he added in a mock-snitchy voice, "Even your friends are morons," and she burst out laughing.

They bumped into each other then, touching, and walked down the street together.

CHAPTER THREE

"I was ready to step in back there . . . in the bus. True. I woulda sorted them out for you."

They were halfway along their street by now, a long, wide stretch of asphalt road and brick homes with wire fences. Alex walked on the inside, closest to the fences, his bag slung casually over one shoulder. It kept slipping down his arm, only to be pushed back up to where it belonged. Marta watched him perform his little bag dance and smiled.

"Oh yeah," she said.

"I would have. They don't scare me."

He grinned at her, showing off, standing to his full height, which barely came up to Marta's neck.

"Swing a punch," said Alex, nimble like a boxer. "Go on, swing. See if you can hit me . . ."

He danced on his toes until his bag slipped off his shoulder and dropped onto his foot. Marta snorted, then looked away. He caught a worried look in her expression. It was a brief flash of another Marta, an interruption to normal programming. Had the idiots on the bus actually bothered her? Screw them, he thought. They weren't worth a glob of spit. She took them too seriously. So what if they cracked jokes about how she looked? That just proved how stupid *they* were.

"You know," said Alex. "That guy, he wouldn't have actually hurt you. They don't hurt girls . . ."

"You're wrong," said Marta, correcting him. "They don't *hit* girls."

Her words were hard, and he kicked at a rock in response, but it bounced back off the fence and hit him in the shin. Hobbling, Alex kicked another rock just to prove he wasn't afraid. This one had the grace not to seek revenge.

"I've got to take a letter to the pastor for my dad," said Marta. "At the church. Want to come with me?"

"But that's down Ferry Street," complained Alex.

"It's not *that* far," she said. "Don't be so lazy. It's only a few extra streets to walk . . ."

"Okay," he said, putting an end to her lecture. "I'm coming . . ."

He had nothing better to do. As they walked he tried to spark up a conversation—light, brainless topics—but Marta still seemed worried and preoccupied. Alex looked at her again, and a cold knot suddenly grew in his stomach. Of course! It had to be the news about the Jockey. She would have heard that he was back. He sped up a little, grabbing a handful of berries from a tree and flicking them along the ground. He wanted to put distance between himself and Marta, because she'd ask. She had to ask. After all, she was one of the few people who knew what the Jockey's return really meant to him.

Eventually he heard Marta puffing behind him. "Alex, wait," she called. He slowed reluctantly, and waited for her to catch up. Marta arrived, brushing her hair from her eyes. "I heard about—" she started, but a barking dog exploded at them from behind a fence. Both jumped, then laughed, watching the dog's snout poke out from a tiny gap under the fence. It had obviously been waiting for an opportunity to ambush.

"I hate the way they do that," said Alex, kicking the fence.

The dog went into hysterics, its bark breaking into a high-pitched squeak.

"I wouldn't do that," said Marta over the din.

"Why not?"

"I saw a guy do something like that and the dog got out through a hole and chased him down the street."

Alex started laughing, imagining the hapless man's surprise when the dog burst free. "What an idiot," he said.

"That's probably what the dog thought, too," said Marta.

They walked on, the dog's protest blending into the background noise. Alex ran ahead a few times to kick stones and stray cans along the street. He wished they could just go back to their usual mode, chatting nonstop, sharing jokes and stories about their day. And arguing.

Not that they ever called it arguing, it was more a form of verbal jousting, trying to outdo each other. They were next-door neighbors, and had been at each other ever since they tottered around in diapers. In the early days, it was Marta who terrorized Alex, pushing him over until he cried, then standing with a half excited, half frightened look on her face until her own tears started to flow.

As they grew older, their forms of communication became more sophisticated. Words and projectiles were tossed from one yard to the other, mostly depending on who was bored. Then midway through primary school, Alex's parents had had their first breakup. He started coming into Marta's yard, sitting on the low fence watching her at play. She loved to invent long, private games on her front porch, and was so absorbed that Alex was not much more than a background detail.

Then he threw suggestions at her for the game, funny solutions for what Marta should do with the troublesome princess (the cat) or the dashing prince (the dog). As she took these on board, Alex started insinuating himself into the games. But then he began forcing the play into new territory. The prince and princess were having marital problems, the knight and the queen were consulting their lawyers. Marta eventually banished him.

They resumed their jousting relationship not long after the Jockey's arrest. Marta started dropping by after school with chocolate biscuits and homework. Alex found that he liked her company, and he liked even better the way she knew all the homework questions. His grades steadily improved, riding as they did on the wave of her intelligence, until he realized that he was working a lot harder than he ever wanted to. He dug his heels in, and their afternoons became more casual, centered around the TV, jokes, and an ever-present packet of chocolate biscuits.

There was always something to laugh about—until today. Alex glanced at his unusually quiet friend, catching her looking at his fat lip out of the corner of her eye.

"You got wetted again," she said.

He was relieved to talk about a familiar subject, and smiled at her description. "Wetted?" he said. "Where'd you get that from?"

"I don't know," said Marta. "Was it Barry Pilsener?"

Alex nodded, then tried to lighten the mood. "That guy is so dumb," he said. "If his brains were dynamite he wouldn't have enough to blow his nose."

Marta laughed. This was an old game. "He's so dumb," she said, "he needs a recipe to make ice cubes."

Alex nodded his head at the insult. He'd run out of berries, so he proceeded to rip as much foliage as he could from the overhanging shrubs along the way.

"You don't have to go near them," said Marta, watching him strip a branch from a small bush with one pull.

"They need me," said Alex. "I'm, like, the best thing in their day. Besides, I'm bored. Most of the guys in my class are stupid and want to kick footballs all day. At least the seniors talk to me . . ."

"That's not *talking* to you!" said Marta.

"Whatever you want to call it," he said, shrugging. "School is so bad. I sit around and it's like . . . like some big dead thing is lying across me. I hate that. You know?"

"So what's that got to do with them?"

Alex grinned at her, a cheeky mischievous look making his face come alive. "They wake me up," he said.

She didn't seem convinced by his explanation.

"Alex," she said quietly next to him.

He tensed. Here it came. The Jockey. She wasn't going to let it go. Should he run again? That was hardly going to work all afternoon. He put his head down and mumbled, "What . . . ?"

"I heard," she said.

"So?"

"Maybe your dad could help?"

Alex turned on her, wild with a brief anger, before snapping, "Don't be stupid."

They were near the church, and he accelerated away, walking up the stone steps until he stopped, suddenly feeling exposed and alone. He waited for Marta to join him, allowing her to enter first.

They stood in the foyer before a set of double glass doors that led to the inside of the church. A service was taking place, and Alex watched the pastor at the front of the congregation, dressed in his long white cassock with gold embroidery on it. He was reading from a black book, his glasses pushed down the end of his nose. Alex walked up to the glass, breathing on it. Why the hell were they all going to church in the middle of the afternoon? Then he saw the coffin at the front of the congregation and he stepped back quickly.

"We'd better go," he said, backing out of the foyer.

"It's okay," said Marta. "I've got to give him the letter . . ."

"But there's dead people in there . . ."

"Only one, silly." Alex glared at Marta and she smiled, saying, "It's just a funeral. Don't tell me you've never seen a dead person before."

"Of course I have," sniffed Alex. "When my old Poppa died, remember? I went to his funeral, it's no big deal. I mean, it's not like I'm scared of dead people or nothing."

"God will strike you down with fire if you lie in his church," said Marta, smiling.

"Oh, gosh," gasped Alex in mock horror. "You'd better get the marshmallows out." He looked back at the church, the coffin so polished, a shining lie in itself. Someone was dead in there, decaying. "It's just . . . you know . . . ," he continued. "What if there's, like, a ghost or something?"

"Alex!"

He shrugged, then counted the mourners packed into the first ten rows of the church. There were at least a hundred of them. What would the dead guy look like now? Did he have a smile on his face? Or was his expression serious? In the movies, dead people always looked like they were sleeping.

"When I was little," he said, "I used to think that all those people who died on TV and stuff, you know, they died for real."

Marta raised her eyebrows. "There'd be a lot of corpses around if that was true."

"Yeah," he said. "But, I think I kinda thought they were all criminals or murderers or something that were waiting to be executed. . . . So they put them in the movies and shot them instead."

Marta looked at him, deadpan, then spoke in a fake, cheerful voice. "Gee, I'm so glad you've grown up now and don't have any more of those dark and depressing thoughts."

"Don't you believe it," said Alex, grinning wickedly at her.

The pastor was having trouble getting his glasses back on his face. The huge sleeves of his garment kept slipping down, covering his hand. In the end, he flung his arm out with a flourish and put his spectacles onto his nose. Nobody clapped or cheered, although Alex felt like giving him at least a whistle for the effort.

Marta stood on her tiptoes now, looking anxiously around the congregation. Alex put his hands in his pocket and leaned against a side wall. The place smelled funny: a mixture of old wood and new carpet. There was a fluorescent light overhead, buzzing incessantly. It was getting on his nerves.

"At last," said Marta.

A woman in the back row of the church had turned and spotted them. She stood and walked quietly into the foyer, taking care to shut the glass doors without making a sound.

"Mrs. Wilson," whispered Marta.

"Marta," said Mrs. Wilson in a hushed voice. Then she gave the girl a long, warm hug.

It went on forever. Alex scuffed his shoes on the carpet. How much longer? It was embarrassing.

"It's so good to see you, beautiful," said the woman.

He stared at the woman. Beautiful? He would describe Marta as a lot of things—funny, smart—beautiful would not be one of them. The embrace finally came to an end, and Marta retrieved an envelope from her schoolbag, handing it to the woman with a quick glance at Alex. He smirked at her and she blushed. Good. She deserved it after leaving him standing there for so long.

"Is this the reference your dad said he'd write?" asked Mrs. Wilson.

Marta nodded. "He said he hoped it was what you wanted."

"I'm sure it is. Could you do me a favor? Ask your dad to order the sausages for Saturday night?"

"Sure," said Marta.

"And I was wondering if I could talk to you later about youth group. . . . ?"

"Okay . . ."

Alex almost groaned on Marta's behalf. What a life she had. Continual groups and church camps and barbecues for the poor or whatever. They might call her "beautiful," but they practically kept her locked up she was so busy with church stuff over the weekend. Blanking out the conversation, he watched the mourners in the church as they all stood. They were going to sing a hymn now. He rolled his eyes.

A muted organ started playing from near the front, its warm

tones swaying out of the dark pews and polished wood. Alex turned his back to the sound, watching as cars flashed past through the church's massive doorway. Then the music lifted, turned into a tide as a hundred voices joined together. It made his skin crawl, the way those voices resonated right through him, urging him to move, to sing along, to shake the dust from the rafters. How they rode the melody, the harmonies, how they gave so much life. Marta stopped, listening, and the woman leaned forward to open the glass doors a crack.

Now the bass male voices escaped, hitting Alex like a blast of wind. He felt his stupid throat tighten, and tried to cover his embarrassment by singing out-of-tune drivel over the top of the voices, until Marta silenced him with a look.

The hymn resonated through the small space, echoing around and around, shaking his rib cage, rattling his heart.

He had an overpowering urge to do something. Anything but just stand there and have this force wash over him. A tear formed in the corner of his eyes, and he turned to Marta, angry with her for bringing him to this place.

"Can we go now?" he snapped, his voice hard and unkind.

Marta started at his rudeness, then nodded, giving the woman a quick hug good-bye. They left the church foyer as the glass doors were closed behind them, the voices lost now, muted by the barrier.

They walked with their heads down, traffic thudding beside them. Alex turned to his friend, an irrational anger rising in him.

"Don't ask me to come to the church again, okay?" he snapped.

"Why?"

"I dunno," he shrugged. "Just don't . . ."

He expected Marta to ask for more of an explanation, but she came to an abrupt halt, then took a sharp intake of breath and hissed, "Shivers!" It was a strong word for her.

Alex saw a look of cold certainty in her eyes as she stared across the street.

"Oh, Alex," she said. "He's following you."

He followed her gaze and saw the Jockey standing on the sidewalk across the street, his face a blank.

CHAPTER FOUR

"**B**ut why would he just be standing there?" said Marta, continuing a discussion that was rapidly turning into another argument. They were almost home by now, having left the church and its precinct behind in a hurry. "Does he live over this way?"

"I dunno," said Alex.

"Because he used to live in Queen's Park—"

"He used to live in lots of places," snapped Alex. "Like prison!"

"I know," mumbled Marta.

Alex banged his schoolbag against the fences as they walked home, hitting it harder and harder with each step. It would have been better if they'd locked the Jockey up forever, but he supposed you'd have to do something really bad, like murder, for that. The Jockey had attacked a policeman with a bat, and that only kept him in for a year.

"Are you sure he wasn't here on purpose?" asked Marta.

Alex wanted to scream. She wasn't going to let it go, was she? "Yes, I'm sure," he mumbled, praying she'd drop it. She didn't.

"I mean," she said, her face twisted with worry, "it seems like an amazing coincidence that he'd be in the same street . . ."

Alex turned on her, furious. "Don't be stupid," he said. "I've told you. Why would the Jockey follow me? I don't mean nothing to him. Right?"

"Sorry, Alex," said Marta. "I wasn't thinking."

He kept walking.

"Alex? I'm sorry?"

She followed, barely able to keep up with his pace. They didn't speak, not even commenting on the barking dog who tried once again to ambush them. They were nearing home—two neat cream-brick houses that stood side by side. Alex lived with his dad in the first of the cream-brick homes, spending every second weekend with his mom and her new husband, Rod, in their tiny flat on the other side of the city. His dad managed an electrical goods shop in the Marble Hill shopping complex, and he usually didn't get home until well after six-thirty.

The second cream-brick bungalow, with the brand-new tiled roof, was Marta's. It would be empty until six. Her dad worked the afternoon shift at the car factory and was always gone by the time she came home. Her mother worked at the supermarket and wouldn't be home until six. Marta's older brother had his own job now.

As they came within a few yards of their homes, Marta broke the long silence between them. "Did he talk to you today?" she asked.

Alex nodded.

"Did he . . . did he ask . . . ?"

Alex walked on. There it was, laid out in the open now. The one thing he'd been wondering all afternoon himself. Would the Jockey ask? Would he want to know what had really happened that evening after they met outside his dad's store? They arrived at Alex's gate, and Marta started to come in with him.

"I got homework," he said, so quickly it sounded harsh.

A brief look of hurt rushed over Marta's face, and she wiped away a strand of hair from her eyes. "What on?"

"Tribes of Africa . . . or something . . . ," mumbled Alex.

"We did that last term. You started yet?"

"I dunno," said Alex. He hated talking about schoolwork at the best of times, but right now it was annoying him to the point of anger. "We had this dumb storyteller today, like, giving us some crap about sneaking up on a lion. If it was me, I'd take a semiautomatic machine gun to the thing. No, even better, a bazooka! Blow its guts across the plain . . ."

"That is so sick," said Marta.

"It's meant to be," said Alex grimly.

Marta sighed. "What if I bring some chocolate biscuits over?"

"Really," he said, "I gotta do my homework and stuff."

He walked down the rest of the driveway, fumbling for his key. As he turned it in the lock he thought he heard her say, "I'll pray for you." She'd still be watching him, standing on the sidewalk with that worried look on her face. He felt like yelling at her, "I'm okay," but that would just hurt her feelings again. And he didn't want to do that.

He went inside and sighed. The house felt cold, even though spring was coming on. There was an awful odor in the air, but Alex didn't feel inclined to find out what was causing it. He looked out through the front windows. She was gone. Alex's dad was always telling him that he wore down his friends. Maybe he was doing that with Marta? He decided that she must be indestructible. That the church gave her a supernatural power to withstand his annoying ways.

He threw his bag inside his room, then retrieved a library book on African tribes from it and went into the living room. Removing a huge pile of clean laundry that he hadn't folded yet, he sat on the couch. The bruise on the back of his leg started throbbing, and it took him several minutes to find a comfortable position.

Twisted into a strange shape, Alex opened the large book and stared at the pictures. They were glossy photos of African men and women in tribal dress: dancing, performing ceremonies, smiling, sharing a joke. He stared at the photos. Young boys, not much older than himself looked back, their faces serious. He imagined one of them might be the character in the story, the young man who had to steal part of a lion's mane. He touched their bright, shining faces, lean and strong, felt the warm wind that blew against their skin, heard the lazy buzzing of the insects around their heads.

Maybe they had hunted a lion, faced down their darkest fear. A lion would not play games with you. It would be swift, brutal, slice you open in half the blinking of an eye.

And pee all over your bones for the pleasure of it . . .

Alex's stomach tightened, and he felt a need to look out of his living-room window at the slowly fading light. The street was empty. Somehow this familiar scene reassured him. Turning the pages of the book at random, he was confronted with slabs of text that blurred before his eyes and made his head spin.

He blamed it on the words, this agitation, and slammed the book onto the glass coffee table, hearing what sounded like a cracking.

"Screw it!" he yelled.

He told himself that if he'd been born with a halfway decent brain then he wouldn't have been in this mess in the first place. It was his faulty head, his inability to read more than a few sentences, that started the dangerous relationship with the Jockey.

Some teacher or librarian must have had a macabre sense of humor, creating a reading program for the slower junior students. Enlisting the help of older students to listen to the younger ones read, a model of peer education, twice a week, with the title, "Reading Partnerships." Partnerships in Crime would have been more appropriate.

Back then, Alex had been excited by who his reading partner would be. The Jockey already had a sizable reputation at school. But their first session together had been a near disaster. Alex wasn't capable of reading anything more complex than the simplest story, so the Jockey had laughed openly at him when he sat down with his basic little text. "Got a baby book . . . ," he chided, grinning unkindly as Alex stumbled over the story in his monotone voice. Page after weary page, until the Jockey ripped the book from him and said that he'd have a turn. And that was when "The Little Thief" was born.

"Once upon a whatever, there's this little guy, right . . . ?" began the Jockey, making it up as he went along.

"What's his name?"

"I dunno. Call him . . . um . . . the Little Thief, okay? So the Little Thief, he's like poor, and he wants stuff all the time. And he figures out how to get it. He cases this department store each night after school, 'cause he's looking for a weakness in the store's security, right? And one night he sees something amazing."

"What is it?"

"It's a light . . . and it's coming from a window, high up. A lazy security guard sits up there and has a smoke or something. Every Wednesday night, this fella leaves the window open. Perfect, eh? The Little Thief is happy, right? He can climb that drain and get to the light. You know, like climb inside. Then he'll be able to get some good stuff, claim his prize. 'Cause he's sick of having nothing but crap at home. Sick of watching other kids with excellent stuff and he's got none . . ."

Alex had sat transfixed, drinking in every word. By the end of the story the Jockey had punched him playfully on the arm and said, "You're all right, aren't ya," and a friendship had been born. From that day on, their reading sessions consisted of the Jockey telling variations on "The Little Thief" story, and his exploits in crime.

Alex stood up from the couch with a yawn and went into the kitchen. It was time for some hunting and gathering. A pile of greasy dirty dishes confronted him, and he realized with a groan where the smell was coming from. Another one of his jobs. He'd tackle the dishes later . . . and the laundry. Removing a packet of chocolate biscuits from the near-empty cupboard, which he had to admit was a lot easier than spearing a lion, he wiped away a pile of crumbs and leftovers from the kitchen table and tried to sit down on a kitchen chair. Once again the bruise plagued him, and he found that the best position was with his legs splayed.

As he pulled the first biscuit from the packet he grimaced, thinking he must look like his old Poppa, who came to live with them for the last couple of years of his life. He'd sit in the same pose on an old, cracked vinyl chair in the middle of the concrete of their backyard, transistor radio on his knee, cup of foul-smelling red wine in his hand. Watching the vegetables, which he grew outside his little shed-home that Alex's father had converted for him. Teeth crooked and yellow, hands callused and cracked from years of hard work, old Poppa would indulge in his favorite sport—criticism.

"Why you let the boy speak to you like that? In my day, they woulda taken the belt buckle to him . . ."

Alex pulled his fourth biscuit from the packet, crunching it angrily as he remembered his grandfather. He was on the fifth when the phone rang. He answered it with a mouthful of crumbs. "Yes," he said, spraying them everywhere.

"It's Mom, darling."

She had that wary tone in her voice, like she thought he was going to explode on the other end of the phone or give her a hard time. Alex hated it when she sounded like that. It never even gave him a chance to be nice.

"Hi," he grunted.

"Listen, could you do me a favor," said his mother, breezy, light. "I can't have you this weekend. Rod has to travel for work and I'm going with him. So can we make it the weekend after?"

Alex rolled his eyes. Coward. She was always doing this, making arrangements through him rather than talk to her ex-husband. Now he'd have to tell his father, and his father would explode, and probably call his mother and it would all end in a monster fight.

"Can't you call Dad at the shop?"

"He's usually busy . . ."

He was silent for a while. Eventually he heard his mother speak.

"Alex?"

"Okay," he said. "I'll tell him."

"You're not disappointed?"

"No."

"How's school?"

"It's fine. The teachers are fine. The work is fine. The weather is fine . . ."

"Alex . . ."

He sighed. Couldn't she take a joke? "I got homework, Mom."

"Oh . . . Well, I . . ."

"See ya." He hung up.

After the first breakup all those years ago, he'd been so desperate to get his parents back together again. He'd lobbied and pleaded until the happy day when his mom came back with her suitcases and stayed a few years longer. By the end of the second great battle of the home, Alex was relieved when his mom pulled the suitcases down from the closet. He didn't care who left, just as long as the fighting stopped. He looked back at the kid he'd once been, the kid who'd prayed for his parents to reunite, and thought what a jerk he had been.

Alex walked back to the couch, picked up the remote, and sat in one smooth action, yelping with pain from the bruise. After some more rearranging, he switched on the TV, put his feet up, and balanced the biscuit packet nicely on his stomach. This was all right. Almost comfortable. There was nothing on, but what did that matter? Alex flicked around the channels, watching mutely, slipping further and further down into the couch. He was almost in a state of torpor when he noticed someone was standing outside his window, looking in. Someone very large.

Barry Pilsener.

CHAPTER FIVE

He couldn't be totally sure, but it seemed as if Barry Pilsener was shouting out that he was furry. Alex turned the TV off and walked cautiously to the window. His tormentor didn't look furry. In fact, he looked slightly crumpled, with his feet planted between the lavender and daisy bushes. The giant's face was a grotesque mix of friendliness and discomfort. Had he managed to impale himself on a garden stake? Standing in a garden bed was not normal behavior for the likes of Barry Pilsener. Nor was shouting that he was furry. If that *was* what he was saying.

The front windows were double-glazed, a special deal his father had arranged with one of the other traders in Marble Hill. Not much noise made it through to the living room. Trucks were reduced to faint rumbles, birds were made mute, and Pilsener's lungs were barely able to produce more than a garbled, muffled sentence about fleece. Alex pointed to his ears and shook his head, shrugging his shoulders for extra effect.

"What are you saying?" he yelled.

A brief wave of frustration passed over Barry's face, before he tried again. With hands cupped around his mouth, the giant shouted, "I'm furry!" again.

Alex rolled his eyes. This was getting ridiculous. He couldn't care less if Barry was furry, hairy, or covered in spots, he wanted him out of his front yard.

"Go away!" he yelled, waving his arm at the Pilsener bulk.

"What?" shouted Barry.

"Go away!"

Barry shook his head. Now *he* couldn't hear. "I . . . fed . . . I . . . furry," he shouted.

Either this was a new trick dreamed up by the senior boys, or Barry had forgotten his medication. Alex looked around to see if anyone else was standing in his garden. The street was empty. The front yard deserted. There was just Barry, with that strange look on his face. Alex examined it a bit closer for clues. Barry's skin seemed flushed, almost blushing, but an uneven blush. One side of his face was redder than the other. And smudged, too. But with what? Were those bruises and abrasions?

A cold chill passed over Alex as he stared at Barry's cheek, the clear imprint of damage left behind on his skin. Then he glanced up further to see that the owner of the bruises was looking him in the eye, a revolting sight made even worse by the fact that Barry was trying to smile. Suddenly, the absurdity of the situation hit Alex. The giant moron looked as if he was holding in an enormous fart. Alex couldn't help himself and he started laughing.

A lightness of mood overtook him, releasing the tension of the day. It was the same buzz he felt when a funny quip came to him. Maybe he should have a bit of fun here, take the game to a new height.

"You're not *that* furry," shouted Alex.

"Huh?" said Barry.

"I said, you're not that furry. You're more hairy . . ."

Barry shook his head, pointing to his ears, which were quite large and rippled.

"I agree," continued Alex. "Those ears are pretty hairy, but it's the nose I'm worried about. Have you ever considered shaving it?"

"No," shouted Barry, although it sounded more like "Mow." He tried once more to pass on the message, then sighed, reaching for his schoolbag, which was lying at his feet.

Alex stopped. Had he gone too far with the hairy jokes? What was in the bag? A gun? A knife? An iron bar? Barry emerged with a notebook and a pen, then proceeded to write something down. He didn't exactly have his tongue hanging out as he wrote, but he did take an awfully long time. Eventually he finished his prose and held it up to the window for Alex to read.

I'm sory.

Even Alex noticed the spelling mistake, but decided not to mention it. Why spoil a good thing? An apology didn't come along every day.

"Can you read it?" shouted Barry several times.

"Yep," replied Alex, once he'd understood the question. Then he nodded his head for emphasis.

Barry nodded back. "Okay?" he shouted.

Alex nodded again, reading Barry's lips. He was becoming quite an expert.

"Okay," said Barry. He shoved his notebook and pen into his bag, slung it over his shoulder, and trudged away, knocking the daisy bush sideways in the process.

What was that all about? Bruisers like Barry were never sorry, unless of course they'd just been caught by a teacher or the cops, and then they were terribly sorry. *"I'm sorry, I'm sorry, I won't do it again . . ."* But no teacher had witnessed Barry's lame attempt at dunking. And even if they had, that wouldn't prompt the moron to stand on the daisies and apologize.

Alex paced around the room. This had a bad smell to it. The smell of conspiracy. The smell of someone with a far better imagination than Barry and his mob. There was a solution to this puzzle, an answer that Alex refused to even consider.

He went into his bedroom and opened his dresser. A tattered old magazine lay at the bottom under a brick. On the cover was a monstrous bodybuilder with bulging muscles. Taking the brick and the magazine into the living room, Alex lay them on the coffee table and turned to page 44. Then he picked up the brick. Biceps first, curling slowly, just like the guy in the magazine advised him. Keep his elbows tucked in, don't bend the back, concentrate on curling up, curling down. One, two, three . . .

Why was Barry put up to a fake apology?

Nine . . . ten . . . eleven . . .

Damn!

He dropped the brick onto the couch and inspected his skinny arms. No change. Just scrawny little sticks with barely enough meat to cover a pencil. Most of the guys his age had muscles, and they never bothered with weights or gyms. It wasn't fair.

Alex sat gingerly on the couch and stared at the bodybuilder in the magazine, whose name was Rocky or Ricky or just plain Rock, he couldn't remember. The photos and words danced about, making him crazy. He dropped the magazine and shouted for the hell of it.

The Jockey had been thinking for sure. All those months after his arrest, waiting for the trial, then his twelve-month sentence inside Barlow Road. Time. Plenty of it. Time to wonder.

Alex closed his eyes. Damn that evening. Damn the fact that he'd been sitting outside his dad's electrical store when he should have been home in bed. Then he wouldn't have run into the Jockey and had *that* conversation. But it was inventory time, and his dad had insisted he stay behind at the shop with him, allowing Alex to sit on the bench outside for fresh air.

The Jockey had been so glad to see Alex. He'd given him a playful box on the arm, asked him what he was doing out here. Alex had explained about the inventory and the endless rattling of his father's computer keyboard, which was driving him nuts. Then the Jockey had sat down.

"Tonight's the night," he'd said.

"What night?" Alex had asked.

"The Little Thief's gonna claim that prize."

Alex had looked at him, puzzled, and the Jockey had laughed.

"It's just a story to you, innit?" And he'd laughed some more, pushing until Alex fought back. They'd wrestled for a while, then the Jockey had sat back again, a serious look on his face. "I don't have a brother or nothing," he'd said. "I'll tell ya what. After I find my window, I'll buy you a CD or maybe even a CD player or something. Come into your old man's store and get it. Tomorrow. Okay?"

Alex had glanced back into the shop at his father, hunched over his laptop with a worried expression on his face. "Yeah, sure," he'd said, thinking nothing more of the Jockey's bragging. Then the Jockey had stood and made his way around the corner.

The next time Alex saw him was in a photograph in the newspaper.

Now he was sitting on a brick on his couch—a fact brought to his attention by an ache in his good leg—wondering how far this dangerous new game would go. He flipped the brick onto the floor, debating his next move, when the doorbell rang.

The move had been made for him.

Shuffling to the front door as softly as he could, Alex checked the visitor's silhouette through the bubbled glass. It was a familiar shape. He retreated to the back door as fast as he could, opening it quietly, but rusty hinges were his undoing. The loud squeak was matched by Alex's own cursing. He slammed the screen door behind him, no need for stealth now, and was about to jump down the steps when he heard the voice he'd been dreading.

"You going out, then?" asked the Jockey.

Alex jumped, despite himself, landing awkwardly on the grass and rolling over onto his back. He tried to look cool as he picked himself up, saying, "No."

"Can I come in?" asked the Jockey, sauntering up in that menacing way he had.

"I don't think so," said Alex.

"But I need medical assistance." He held up his hands, showing cuts and scrapes across both sets of knuckles. He grinned broadly, then added, "I fell over."

There was only one thing that made knuckles bleed like that. And that was one thing the Jockey was too good at. Everyone kept well away from him because of it. But sometimes there was no escape.

Ask Barry.

He climbed back up the steps and opened the back door, feeling so sick he thought he might burp or throw up all over the place.

"It's been a long time, Alex," said the Jockey as he sauntered in, making his way to the living room as if he knew the place well. Flopping dramatically onto the couch, he gave him a cold smile as Alex followed him into the room.

"Let's talk about the good old days. I've missed you."

CHAPTER SIX

"I thought you were in Queensland," said Alex, throwing the Band-Aid wrappers into the trash.

The Jockey sat admiring his newly covered knuckles. "Came back," he muttered. Then he looked up at Alex and said, "Can't figure out what happened to you. You used to be such a cool kid."

Alex smiled grimly. He could see the Jockey's muscles ripple under his shirt. If anyone had changed, it was him. He was no longer a kid. Twelve months behind bars would do that to a person. There was an air about him that reeked of danger, with his shaved head and his hard, mean exterior.

The brick lay on the floor, and the Jockey rolled it around with his foot, as if it were perfectly natural to have a brick on your living-room floor. "Watcha reading?" he asked, sitting forward violently and grabbing the book about African tribes from the table. "Check out these guys," he said, flicking through the pages.

"Look," said Alex. "My dad will be home soon. You'd better go . . ."

"Your dad won't be home until after six." The Jockey flicked through the book, not stopping at any particular page. "So," he eventually said. "Still into little kids' stories, eh? Only you gotta have a storyteller now."

Alex blushed, and leaped instantly to the defense of the actor and his tale. "He wasn't all that bad. . . . A bit babyish, but it was an okay story about a dude who had to sneak up on a lion and stuff . . . you know . . . to prove he was a man and all that." Then he added, "If it was me, I'd use a bazooka, blow the lion's guts away."

The Jockey was even less impressed by the joke than Marta had been, giving Alex a withering look. He shook his head slowly, then continued to flick through the book. Finally he stopped at a page and showed Alex a photograph of a young man with a dead animal stuck to the end of his spear. "Do you think this guy ate that thing? Eh?"

"I dunno," shrugged Alex.

"Better than some of the crap I had to eat in Barlow Road."

There it was. The first mention of *that* subject. Barlow Road. Juvenile Detention Center for wayward young men. A bland name for what everyone knew was essentially a prison for boys. Alex sat down on a stool, then stood up again, unable to decide what to do next. The Jockey smiled at him, enjoying his discomfort.

"You got no idea what to make of me, have ya?" he said. "Relax, don't be so nervous. I haven't changed that much. We used to be old mates, eh? Reading buddies. Have you forgotten?"

Alex shook his head. No, he hadn't forgotten about The Little Thief story. He looked at the Jockey now, still "little," but carrying around a reputation larger than life.

"So," said the Jockey, placing his leg up on the couch. "You've been taking on the big boys. They call you the 'Grub,' eh? 'The Lip' is more like it. Or maybe just plain 'Smart Alex.' They give you plenty of grief, from what I hear. I don't get it. Why fight 'em when you know you're gonna lose?"

"Who says I lose?" said Alex.

"Me," said the Jockey, staring at him. "I thought you were tougher than that."

"It's just something we do . . . you know?" he said, trying to make light of the topic. "I, like, tell them how stupid they are. And then Barry tries to dunk me. He uses the same toilet every time, and he never gets me wet. I guess that proves I'm right, eh? Besides, it beats watching the ants eat stale sandwiches."

"And you think that makes you better than them?"

"I *know* it does," said Alex.

"Who did you say was stupid again?" asked the Jockey.

Alex didn't answer. The Jockey waved the spear photograph at Alex. "Imagine trying to dunk this character?" he said. "You'd get a frigging spear in your heart before you made the first move." He flung the book onto the table and sighed dramatically. "What the hell am I gonna do with you? I mean, look at ya. Didn't I teach you nothing? Didn't I ever tell ya about making a difference? All you ever seem to make is a frigging comedy show. Listen to me, little Alex. You open your mouth to say something, you gotta mean it, right? You clench your fist to straighten someone out, you gotta frigging *hurt* them."

There was a harsh edge to the Jockey's voice, matched by his eyes. Alex imagined being cornered by those eyes in a dark place.

They would reflect everything about you in their steel, their coldness. They would expose your frailty, then divulge your doom. Alex shivered, rubbing his legs, looking anywhere but at the Jockey's face.

"I used to think about you inside," said the Jockey, relaxing his tensed body.

"Oh," said Alex. "Um . . . right." Then he added, "About that . . ." But his voice trailed off into nothing.

"About what?" said the Jockey.

"Nothing . . . about inside . . ."

"What the hell would you know about inside?" said the Jockey, the harshness back in his voice. "Seen a TV show about prison, have ya? Think you know what it's like?"

"No, I . . ."

"It was a living hell, Alex. That what you wanna hear? That they beat me every other night? That they hit me with iron bars? Is that what you seen on TV? Sniveling little boys crying for Mama? Praying on their knees?" The Jockey suddenly burst out laughing, as if he'd cracked an enormously funny joke. He wiped tears from his eyes, shaking his head at Alex who sat with a stunned expression. "Barlow Road made me," he said, once his mirth had died down a little. "Hear that? It made me. I was a wet, pathetic little prick before I went in there. Do I look pathetic to you now?"

Alex shook his head. The Jockey nodded, then stared off into the distance, lost in some private thought or memory. He looked at Alex, a strange calm on his face. "Sometimes you don't realize how tough you are until you've been tested."

Alex tried to imagine how the Jockey had been tested inside Barlow Road. Whatever had happened, he looked like he passed with flying colors. If he'd been scary before he went inside, then he was a hundred times more dangerous now that he was out. There wouldn't be too many around who'd take him on.

"So, you were thinking about me while I was on the inside, then, little Alex?" said the Jockey, his voice almost a whisper.

It was all Alex could do to nod. He wiped his palms on his pants. Yes, he'd been thinking about the Jockey, almost every day, imagining him lying on a bunk bed in a darkened cell. And what did he see the Jockey do in this imaginary cell? Think. Play a movie in his head. The same scene over and over again. In this scene, the Jockey sees himself leave Alex that night outside the electrical store and walk around the corner to find the window. Then he sees Alex get up and walk back into his father's shop, bored—a young, dumb kid, who didn't know any better.

It was a movie that Alex had played a million times in his own head. The difference was, he had actually lived it. He always wished he could change the dialogue in this movie, alter the course of events, but it played out the same every time. His father looking up at him from the computer, asking: "Who were you talking to out there?"

Alex shrugging, saying, "Just a kid from school."

"He looks older than you."

"He's the Jockey. His real name's Darren, only no one ever calls him that. He's all talk, you know, tries to be tough."

"Hm? Like what?"

"You know. Says he's gonna make big money and all that."

His father looks up at this stage in the movie, with a thoughtful expression. Then he says, "What's he doing out here at night?"

Alex is evasive, looks away. "I dunno," he says.

"Alex."

"I dunno."

The silence. The look that Alex knows he can never squirm out of.

"He just went on about finding a window and stuff. But it's all talk. Says it's around the corner . . ."

"Say that again?"

"It's just a story, Dad."

And the music swells in this miserable movie, the dialogue fades away so that the camera can concentrate on the angry, frightened, determined faces: his father interrogating, asking more and more questions; Alex evasive, before finally telling all; his father now picking up the telephone.

Smash cut the music out of there, up comes the sound of Alex, yelling, "What are you doing?" His father holds his hand up, then talks into the receiver, "I'd like to report a possible burglary," and Alex cries out, "Why did you do that?"

Now, almost two years later, it's a question he still can't fathom the answer to. What business was it of his father's to call the police and report on the Jockey? It wasn't his shop that was being robbed. If he'd left it all alone then the cops wouldn't have gone into the store, wouldn't have discovered the Jockey, and the fight would never have taken place. Instead, a police officer lay in the hospital for weeks, belted senseless by a bat, and the Jockey was locked away waiting for his trial, then locked away again in a place where he had a file, a caseworker, and a home full of angry young criminals.

And now he was back. Alex looked at the Jockey. What did he know? One thing was for sure, the movie hadn't ended with that miserable little scene in his father's shop. It was still playing out, right here in his living room.

The Jockey leaned over and picked up the brick, then he

stood, tossing it from side to side. "Ever had to catch a brick?" he said.

Alex shook his head, his eyes locked on the Jockey's hand. It would hurt if he threw it, crack a bone, cut open skin.

"Hard thing to catch for sure," said the Jockey, a sly grin on his face. Then he threw a fake pass at Alex, the brick still in his hand, but the effect was as impressive as if he'd actually thrown the thing.

Alex flung his hands up for protection, banging his head against the wall, then slipping from the stool and landing heavily on his backside. He sat on the ground, his bottom aching, as the Jockey fell onto the couch and rolled around in stitches.

"Look at you," said the Jockey through gasps and gales of laughter. "Look at you."

Alex stood up, trying to regain some dignity. All the times he'd been dunked and laughed at were nothing compared to this. The Jockey had made him feel so small and stupid. Eventually the older boy regained control over himself and stood up, shaking his head.

"How did you get to be such a chicken?" he said. "You used to be cool."

"Hey, it's not like I'm dead or nothing," said Alex, annoyed.

The Jockey smiled. "Whoo! Fighting back, are ya? Got anything else you wanna say?"

"No."

"Too bad. I thought for a moment there you might actually be sick of the taste of piss water . . ."

"Shut up!" shouted Alex, regretting it instantly.

Now the Jockey smiled openly, walking over to Alex and placing his meaty arm around his shoulders. "I always used to reckon you were as close to me as a little brother. You know that? The truth. Don't be a chicken anymore. Okay? I don't like seeing that. And don't be scared of me. We're square, you and me. I've only been to prison, that's all. I'm not some kind of monster, or nothing."

Alex looked up at the Jockey. Surely this was a trick? Something to make him relax before he was hurt? But then again, the Jockey didn't need anyone to be relaxed before he hurt them.

"Why are you being so nice to me?" asked Alex.

"It's like I said. You're my little bro."

"Is that why you . . . you know . . . with Barry?"

The Jockey smiled. "Barry was disrespectful to me. He wouldn't apologize when I asked him."

"Oh . . . so you . . ."

"You want me to color it in for you with crayons?"

Alex shook his head. Could it really be as simple as that? That they'd slip back into the old ways? The Jockey protective again? Wanting to look after "little Alex" by forcing thugs like Barry Pilsener to be nice? Alex smiled. It wouldn't be such an awful life. To have an enforcer like the Jockey on his side.

Then he looked at his guardian angel, at the shaved head showing cuts from the razor, at his grazed knuckles, at the menace that always burned in his eyes, and he shuddered slightly.

"So . . . what happens now?" asked Alex, fearful of what the Jockey's answer might be.

"Now?" said the Jockey. "Well, you owe me . . ."

"Oh," said Alex, his throat suddenly constricting. Owed him what? His loyalty? His life?

The Jockey burst into laughter again, slapping Alex on the back and nearly knocking his shoulder blade out. "You're such a goofy little kid," he said. "I was only fooling with ya. You don't owe me nothing. But I can't look after your interests for you all the time. I got me own life to live."

"Right," said Alex. "That's fine . . ."

The Jockey walked back to the couch and was about to sit down when he turned suddenly, clapping his hands together. "I just had a brilliant frigging idea," he cried.

Alex looked at him warily. "Yeah? What?"

"I'm gonna teach you to stand up for yourself. That's what big brothers do, eh?"

Alex shook his head. No, that wouldn't work for him. He couldn't be tough like that. He'd learned how to be smart and quick and annoying . . .

"Some stage or another you've gotta spit your fears in the eye," said the Jockey.

"Couldn't I just spit Barry Pilsener in the eye instead?"

"This is gonna be beautiful. We'll be like that fella in your African story . . ."

"What?" said Alex. "We'll find a lion?"

"No. Different. We'll go live in the wilderness and survive on our wits. No money, no food. Just our skills. That'll make a man of ya."

"Wilderness?" cried Alex. "What? You mean, go to the country or something?"

"No, moron. The wilderness is in the city."

Now Alex was totally confused. What was the Jockey talking about? The zoo? Perhaps he really did mean to find a lion. He shrugged at the older boy, bewildered, and received a sarcastic roll of the eyes in response.

"The whole frigging city is a wilderness," said the Jockey slowly, as if talking to a baby. Then his eyes lit up with a chilling light, and he launched into a bedtime story of sorts. "Two A.M., you got gangs roaming the back alleys that'll tear you to pieces for looking at them the wrong way. Three A.M., the criminals come out to do their dirty work. Four A.M., when you're feeling the sleepiest, that's when it's the deadliest. That's our wilderness, Alex. You're gonna stay in the city all weekend with no money and no food. You're gonna rely on your brains and your guts and your fists to survive. I've done it, and it's so cool. Nobody's gonna respect you if you stick your head in a toilet. Don't matter how funny you are. You gotta prove yourself against something scary. You gotta face it, Alex. You gotta face death even, and you gotta come through."

"Alone?"

The Jockey smiled, then motioned for Alex to sit down. "Not alone," he said. "I'll be there to show ya. Come on, we got some planning to do. We're gonna sleep rough for the weekend."

CHAPTER SEVEN

He sat in the fading light of his living room long after the Jockey had gone. Replayed everything a hundred times over to see if he could spot the catch, the trick, the nasty surprise that surely must be there.

He couldn't.

The Jockey had left in high spirits, grabbing him in a friendly headlock at the front porch, laughing, saying this was going to be so cool. But Alex couldn't relax into the play-fight, he was jumpy, expecting a sly hit any second. The Jockey didn't seem to notice. He'd left with a promise to follow up on the idea tomorrow, to make plans for their weekend in the city.

Was it true, then? The Jockey didn't suspect him? Hadn't figured out who'd tipped off the police that night? Alex resisted yelling with relief or getting up and going psycho around the room. All these months and it was not an issue. No need to have worried, to have thought about him inside. The Jockey was back.

With a dangerous plan.

Could he do it? Go into the city without money or food and survive on his wits for the weekend? The idea scared the life out of him, but there was no way he'd show that. He didn't want to be laughed at or called a baby. Besides, what could go wrong with the Jockey there?

And it would be a test.

There was something amazingly appealing about facing up to a danger like that and coming through. Then he'd really have something to shove in Barry Pilsener's ugly face. "Look what I did. Me and the Jockey." Imagine that. They'd have to take notice then.

What a moment that would be. He allowed it to play in his imagination, enjoyed the tingle of it, the joy of shoving it in Barry's face, "Hey Barry, gotta love me now . . .," the buzz of walking through the yard, earning respect, having your own space in the crowd, a path that *you* cut through the mass of deadheads around you.

The front doorbell rang. For a second he thought it might be the Jockey returning with bad news. Then he realized who it was.

Alex turned on the lights and opened the door, not surprised at all to see Marta standing on the porch with a plate of hot food and a nervous smile on her face. He'd spotted her through her kitchen window when he was showing the Jockey out. She'd squealed when she'd seen who he was with. Any other time he would have laughed, but he was too distracted at the time to take much notice of it.

She wouldn't know about their little scheme. He liked that, having a real secret from her. Marta knew almost everything else, including the story about his father and the phone call. She'd been the only person he'd told. And she'd kept the secret well, like a good friend would.

He looked down at the plate to see it was pierogi, steaming hot cheese and potato dumplings. "Come in," he said, grabbing a pierogi and stuffing it into his mouth right away, ignoring her warning that they were hot. His tongue screamed in pain and he rushed to the sink, drinking down mouthful after mouthful of water, stalling for time because he knew that eventually she'd ask why the Jockey had come over.

What business was it of hers? She wasn't his mother or guardian angel or whatever she thought she was. He glanced at her, standing with the plate in her hand, a self-righteous smile on her face. Alex was aware that he'd just played out the whole drama of their relationship—she warning him, and he ignoring her. She always knew the *right* thing to do. Sometimes he thought of her as "poor Marta," not for what the dummies at school taunted her about but because of the small world she lived in. Her only other friends were kids from the church, and the only social functions she ever went to were church ones.

Alex's stomach felt bloated now from his drinking, and the thought of another drop of water made him feel ill. He waddled back into the living room, and Marta just came out with it.

"What's going on?" she asked.

Alex shrugged, not sure whether to act dumb or not, then deciding it would simply save time to get on with the interrogation. "Nothing," he said. "Really. We're all cool. He doesn't know nothing. He said so, sort of. We're square, that's what he said."

He knew he had an evasive tone in his voice and was sure that she wouldn't be convinced by his explanation. He wasn't all that convinced himself. She'd think that the Jockey had threatened him to keep him quiet. She'd assume that he was somehow compromised, held to a dangerous bargain for fear of being beaten up. And maybe he, too, would have thought something like that, before the visit.

Marta looked at him suspiciously, then said, "Alex, please. What's really going on?"

"Nothing."

"Please."

"I can't tell you . . ."

"Alex!"

"I can't. He'd kill me. Just a little plan, nothing bad or illegal, so don't worry . . ."

He cursed himself. How easy was that? He'd have to be a lot tougher than this if he was ever going to change. A few questions from Marta and he almost blurted it all out. Now she was on to him.

"When?" she asked.

"Marta. I'm not telling you . . ."

"You have to."

"No, I don't."

"What about your dad?" she said. "Maybe he *could* help this time . . ."

He felt like shaking her, forcing her to see how the world really worked. She was so certain that calling on a parent or a pastor or a woman who called you "beautiful" was going to make a difference. Why couldn't she see that they just screwed everything up?

"My whole life went down the frigging toilet the last time my father helped me," he said. "And you want to make it all happen again?"

"I think what your dad did was really brave," said Marta.

"Oh, right. You would."

"What's that mean?"

"What's it mean?" shouted Alex. "Why don't you ask God the next time you call him on the heaven-phone, or whatever you use? 'Hello, God . . . ?' Oops, sorry, no answer. He's on the frigging toilet . . ."

"Don't be a jerk," said Marta.

"They've just got you fooled, Marta. You want to walk tall around here, you go with the strength. I saw Barry Pilsener stand in my garden and say 'sorry.' Can you believe that? Who do you think made that happen? *He* did."

Marta stared at him, then said, "Look at you. You're all happy and excited. How can he do that to you? After only one afternoon?"

"Shut up," said Alex, turning away from her searching eyes. They seemed to know something about him that even he couldn't see.

"You can't trust him again," pleaded Marta. "You can't. He's horrible. He hurt a man. You can't let him talk you into anything . . ."

"All right!" said Alex, pacing around the room. "Just stop, okay? I'm not a little kid anymore. I know what I'm doing. Just stop crying."

Marta wiped her face, surprised to find her hand wet from tears. She went into the kitchen and started transferring the pierogi from her plate to one of Alex's, sniffing every now and then. He watched her with his stomach as tight as a balled fist, hating himself for what he'd said to her. All the jerks and dickheads at school couldn't hurt her as much as he could. He knew what the Jockey would tell him to do, cut her loose, she was the past, not the way forward.

Alex walked into the kitchen and leaned up against a bench, wanting to say something, but words wouldn't come into his head. He wasn't smart like her. He didn't know the right thing to say in moments like these. "Marta," he said eventually. "I'm . . . sorry . . . okay? For what I said about your church. It's just that . . . I don't understand what you get outa the whole thing."

Marta closed her eyes and tensed. "Please," she said.

"No, I'm not kidding around . . . I really want to know. What is it about the place . . . ?"

"It's not the place," said Marta, washing her plate under some running water, her back to him.

She seemed intent on removing the pattern from the plate, rubbing and rubbing at it with her hand. Alex wanted to rip it from her, make her see he didn't mean to hurt her before. He hated the way she stood there.

"Marta," he said.

"What?" she snapped.

"Come on . . . You know, like, if it's not the place, then what? Talk to me . . ."

She turned, her eyes red, and shook her head. "I don't think you'd understand," she said, then she launched into an explanation, anyway. "I like my pastor, Mr. Wilson, the stuff he says. I like the people there and the services. All that, okay?"

She was still defensive, angry, but Alex was truly interested now.

"But," he said, "how does that help? The people and the services and all?"

"It just does," she said. "I knew you wouldn't get it. The church is where . . . you know . . . where God can see me."

Alex snorted, he couldn't help himself. Where God could see her? Was that it? He relaxed back into his old mode.

"Like, God can't see you in other places?" he said. "What's that supposed to mean? You're hiding at school . . . ?" His voice trailed off. Marta was giving him a strange look. A half knowing, half amused expression on her face. "What?" he said.

"You should know all about hiding yourself at school," she said.

He leaped into the gap between her words and his reaction before she had a chance to see how they'd hit their mark.

"I mean it," he said. "How do you know He can see you?"

"Because I feel it," she said, raising her voice. "In here." She pointed to her heart.

"When? Now?"

"Yes," she said quietly. "I feel it when I know people love me. And when I . . . I care for other people. Haven't you ever felt something like that, too?"

"I don't care about anyone," said Alex flatly.

Marta's face fell. She turned back to the sink, quiet before finally saying, "I don't believe you, Alex Pimentino."

They heard the sound of a key in the front door lock, and Alex's father stepped in from the cold. He sniffed the air, screwing his nose up. "What's that smell?" he asked.

"I brought some food over," answered Marta, wiping her eyes. She still had her back turned.

"No, not that," said Mr. Pimentino, oblivious to Marta's tears. "Something stinks." He stalked into the kitchen and saw the dishes stacked next to the sink. "Alex!" he yelled.

Alex rolled his eyes.

"Can't you just do a simple job when I ask you? Is it too much? Hey? I work really hard, and it's horrible to come home to this." He waved his hand at the dishes.

"Marta made some pierogis," said Alex, hoping to placate him.

"Thank you, Marta," snapped Mr. Pimentino. "I'm sure they're delicious."

"I'd better be going," said Marta. "Mom will be home soon."

"Bye," said Mr. Pimentino, glaring at his son.

Alex walked Marta to the door, but she left without turning back or saying good-bye. He watched her go down the driveway, then went inside. The minute he came into the kitchen his father attacked again, pointing to the dishes, shouting about responsibilities. Alex suddenly exploded back, "What does it matter? They're only dishes!"

"They're more than that," shouted his father. "Do you want to turn into a no-hoper? Become one of the useless slobs who hang around the shopping center?"

"I'm not useless!" yelled Alex.

"No? Well, you're doing a very good impersonation of it at the moment. In my day I would never have ignored a job . . ."

Alex shook his head. "Do you have any idea how much you sound like old Poppa?" he said. "Give me a break."

There was a brief show of surprise in his father's face, then it hardened into a familiar expression—one Alex had seen many times before, whenever old Poppa was criticizing. And old Poppa's list of targets to criticize was vast: his son, his grandson, his daughter-in-law, the whole family, the tomatoes, in fact anything that came within range. Yes, Alex knew that expression on his father's face well, a mixture of grit and hatred. Was that all it came down to for a father and son? After all their years together? A barely concealed expression of contempt?

Alex walked over to the sink and looked at the pile of dishes, covered in old food that had hardened on the plates, crusty remnants of past meals. What a screwup of a day it had been. Marta's tears, the Jockey's plan, and now his father was turning into that miserable old man who had haunted their lives from the shed out the back. He turned on the hot water, a grim, set expression on his face. "I'll do the dishes," he said, wanting to add, "seeing as they're so important . . ."

After a minute his father joined him, and Alex tensed. But a tea towel was dangled before his eyes.

"You dry, I'll wash," said his dad.

Alex didn't look at him, frightened that he might turn back into that Poppa-dad again. He took the tea towel and said, "You sure?"

His father gave a quick chuckle. "Yeah, you're a hopeless washer, anyway."

"Cool by me," said Alex. He stepped away, noticing the softening in his dad. "I'm a hopeless folder of clothes, too," he added. "And my vacuuming sucks . . ."

"Don't push it, boy," said his father, pulling a plate out of the water and slotting it into the rack.

They were silent for a while, the only sound the sloshing of the water and clinking of crockery. Then his father said, "Pierogi for dinner. Polish dumplings for a couple of Italian boys."

Alex nodded. "Do you think old Poppa would approve?" he said.

His dad paused, hands plunged deep into the water, eyes far away. Alex looked at the tight bend in his father's wiry back, tense over the sink, as if he was worried the shadows might attack him. Pulling a knife from the suds and washing it harder than it needed, he turned to Alex with a grim half smile on his face, and muttered quietly, "Who cares, eh? Who gives a frigging damn."

CHAPTER EIGHT

The next morning Alex was certain the whole sleep-rough idea was pure insanity. How could he survive on his wits in the city? He wasn't like the Jockey, he hadn't been hardened by twelve months inside. What if a fight broke out? What if he was separated from the Jockey? He'd be hopeless.

He grabbed a quick breakfast, offered a few grunts in response to his dad's grunts, then packed his bag. His father looked as though he hadn't slept all that well last night. It was no wonder. Alex had woken in the middle of the night, unsettled, with crazy thoughts stirring in his head. He'd tried to go back to sleep but couldn't shake off a nightmarish image of himself alone, the whole world having died in their sleep. Just him to wander the streets. It was horrible.

And then he'd thought, what if it was the other way around? That *he'd* been the one to die. That was when he'd got up and walked down the hall. He went to the master bedroom where he could hear his father snoring.

Alex stood in the doorway until his dad let out a tremendous snort and opened his eyes. He focused on Alex's shape for a brief moment, then yelled in a dreamless fright.

"What?! What! What are you . . . ?"

"It's okay! It's okay!" said Alex. "It's only me."

His father stared at him with blank eyes, trying to make sense of his son's form in the doorway. Then he sighed, and said, "God. I thought you were a ghost or something."

It hadn't been any easier going back to bed after that comment. Eventually sleep had come to Alex, and no doubt to his father, but much later by the look of him.

Alex slung his bag over his shoulder and shouted good-bye, then left for the bus stop. He wasn't surprised that there was no sign of Marta heading for the morning bus. She went home upset, and her mother would have blamed it on him. He was blamed for most things. Alex had heard Marta's mother go on about his un-Christian influence. She probably drove Marta to school to keep her away from the bad boy next door.

He looked at his watch and realized that he was a few minutes late for the bus. Running with a heavy bag was hard enough, but running with his sloppy bag that kept slipping was a nightmare. Alex reached the bus stop just as the bus doors were closing and the driver was preparing to pull away. He banged on the closed doors, his bag down around his elbows. The driver glared at him.

"Aw, come on," yelled Alex through the doors. "I'll be late."

The driver checked his side mirror, then turned back to Alex, opening the doors as a steady stream of cars rushed past on the other side.

"You were lucky the traffic was busy," muttered the driver as Alex trudged on, pulling his bag back from his arms.

All the seats were taken, so he stood in the aisle, praying his bag wouldn't slip and brain the big kid beneath him whose head was perilously close. Some of the seniors sitting in the backseat were eyeing him. They didn't look all that pleased with him. Alex groaned.

Barry Pilsener.

They'd obviously heard about the apology, or at least about the events leading up to the apology. Every now and then the seniors would turn to one another and mutter darkly, then give him even darker looks. They were going to make him pay for Barry's humiliation. And where was the Jockey? Nowhere. Alex smiled grimly. He was alone again, struggling with problems that he hadn't even created.

Two of the seniors stood, and Alex tensed. The bus was several stops from the school. They made their way down the aisle, keeping their eye on him, no smiles, no showing off. They looked deadly serious.

Alex glanced back down at the driver and wondered about getting closer. The first of the seniors pushed past Alex roughly, standing on his toe on the way through. No words were exchanged. He pulled back as the second senior passed, but the thug still managed to kick him in the shin as he went by. Luckily there wasn't enough space to really land a blow, but even so, Alex's leg throbbed with the pain. He didn't let them see it. No point in getting them excited. This wasn't over. Not yet. These friendly little gestures were a warm-up to the main event. It was all improvised, a spur-of-the-moment response to what had happened to their mate.

A host of possibilities ran through Alex's head. Would they act when the bus pulled in at school? Take him off and drag him around the corner, perhaps? His only hope was to somehow try to run, but it was nearly impossible now that the two seniors had parked themselves between him and the door.

Some of the giants in the backseat stood now, making their way down toward him. Other kids on the bus instinctively pulled away, allowing the aggressors some space around him.

"Great," muttered Alex.

None of the seniors looked at him. None winked or smiled or made any passing joke, yet he knew he was the center of their attention. Alex glanced out the window, they were close to the school now. Should he cry out? Shout to the driver? Or would that only postpone the inevitable?

His bag slipped down his arms and he pulled it back up irritably. That was all he needed, a heavy bag to pin him down as the punches started flying. If they started . . .

The bus came to a halt all too soon, and Alex looked out the window to see that they'd arrived at school. The two seniors at the front moved closer to him, smiling, and he could feel the others crowd him from behind. Now what? Were they going to squash him like a fly?

"Hey, you guys stink real bad," said Alex. "So move back, okay?"

"You'll stink even worse, Grub," said the closest senior.

"That's right," added another. "All dead things stink."

Some of the kids at the back of the bus started complaining about the blocked aisle, calling for them to move on, so the seniors shuffled toward the door, Alex firmly wedged between them.

"What is this?" said Alex. "A bit of man-on-man loving or something?"

It earned him a quick jab in the ribs, enough to throb badly. "Shut up."

"Where's your tough guy now?" asked a voice, perhaps in front of him, perhaps behind.

They moved faster now, Alex wedged between, his feet slipping along, stumbling down the steps. He twisted his ankle slightly and a sharp pain shot through to the bone.

"Thanks for the ride, guys," said Alex, the minute they hit the outside air. "But, gotta get to class . . ."

A large foot landed on his, pinning him to the ground. It started to hurt, then hurt more, until tears formed in Alex's eyes.

"Sniveling little snot," said the owner of the foot, an ogre not much smaller than the giant Pilsener.

"Say sorry," whispered a voice.

Alex shook his head, and the pain in his foot escalated until he buckled at the knees. He could smell them, their anger, their hatred.

"Say sorry."

Alex shook his head again. Gasped. He had nothing to be sorry for. They could crush him into the dirt, but he hadn't done a thing wrong.

"Say . . ."

The voice didn't finish its order. There was a sudden eruption of shouts, and the pack moved one way, then another. Loud swearing accompanied each sway, until a familiar voice spoke close to Alex.

"Say sorry, snot-brain."

It was the Jockey.

Suddenly the pain in Alex's foot eased, and his large companion with the clumsy boots stepped back a few paces, clutching his stomach.

"I don't know what's wrong with you guys," said the Jockey,

hands on hips, addressing the seniors as if they were a bunch of naughty boys. "I mean, where's yer frigging manners and all?"

They glared at the Jockey, five, six, seven of them, larger boys who had him surrounded, their bodies keen and sharp like waiting spears. With a combined effort they could rush him and bring him to the ground. Not even the Jockey could take on this many. Alex watched them, his eyes darting from one face to the other, looking for signs of attack. But they lowered their gaze or averted their eyes, then bent to pick up bags and left the scene. Alex smiled as they walked off into the yard, vanishing into the buildings. Even after they were long gone, he stood there, the pain in his foot a dull ache, the pain in his ankle almost gone.

His heart still raced, but this time with a wild excitement. "I still didn't hear you say sorry," he yelled, but his taunt fell on shadows and empty spaces.

He turned quickly and wanted to whoop out a victory chant, but the Jockey had vanished. Alex was alone again at the center of the world.

Then the bell sounded.

He caught sight of the Jockey at lunchtime, outside the fence on the sports field. Alex ran in his direction. Even now he could feel it, the same space he'd felt that morning at recess. Running through bunches of kids and games of handball and packs of gatherers, he felt as if he could draw a line across any part of the yard and it would be his line, his corridor that no one else would dare step into.

He could see kids looking at him, too, watching him from a distance. But it wasn't hatred in their eyes or laughter or contempt. They regarded him with some kind of new emotion, as if he now meant something.

"Watcha up to?" asked the Jockey when he arrived at the fence.

"Nothing much. What happened to you this morning?" said Alex. "How come you didn't go to school?"

"Had work to do," said the Jockey, grinning at him.

"Oh yeah? What kind of work . . ."

The Jockey didn't answer, just looked at the packs of kids in the background with disdain, shaking his head. "Don't know why they bother. Not gonna learn nothing in this dump." He turned to Alex. "You figured out what you're gonna say to your old man, yet?"

"About what?" said Alex.

"About the weekend, moron."

"Oh, no."

"You gonna think of something?"

"Yeah . . . I guess."

"You guess?" The Jockey leaned over the fence and took hold of Alex's head in his meaty hands. "You frigging guess? What kind of a weak, dribbly little baby answer is that?" Then he gave him a friendly tap on the back of the head.

Alex shrugged, grinned sheepishly, then said he'd do it when the time was right. The Jockey lifted a backpack from between his feet and reached into it, taking out a black denim jacket.

"This fit you?" he said, handing it over.

"Dunno," said Alex.

"Well, try it on, brick-brain," said the Jockey.

Alex slipped the jacket on, feeling its cardboard tags dig into the back of his neck. The jacket was brand-new, fresh off the clothes rack.

"How'd you . . . like . . . where did this come from?"

"Fell from the frigging heavens," said the Jockey. "You want it or not? Gonna need something to keep you warm this weekend, eh?"

Alex nodded, then sat on the top of the fence still wearing the jacket, kicking the wire with his feet. The tags became increasingly annoying, so he jumped off and ripped them from the jacket, whistling when he saw the price. Something told him that the Jockey hadn't paid for it.

They leaned on the fence, doing nothing much in particular, when the Jockey turned to Alex and said, "You're afraid of your old man, aren't ya?"

It was such a sudden and unexpected question that Alex blushed. "No," he said.

The Jockey grinned. "Yeah, you are. Daddy got you all tied up. Got you looking over your shoulder . . ." Then he placed his hand on Alex's back, not hard, just a friendly gesture. He patted Alex gently, then let go, saying, "Yer a good little kid. Man, this weekend it's gonna be so cool. We're gonna tear the place apart, eh?"

"Yeah," said Alex, feeling his heart race again. This time it was a welcome feeling.

Later, when the bell had sounded and the Jockey had gone, Alex was about to go back to class when he saw an advertising flyer on the ground where the Jockey had been standing. Something about it caught his eye, and he bent over the fence to get a better look. It was a flyer from his father's shop, showing digital cameras and DVD players and plasma TVs. A strange, cold sensation came over Alex, and he looked around to see if there were more of the flyers lying about.

The sidewalk was clean.

He crumpled the flyer up into a ball and dropped it over the fence, then ran into class.

His father was home from work later than usual, and Alex found himself glancing at the clock, wondering what was keeping him. Paranoid thoughts bounced about in his head, all leading to trouble for him with the Jockey's name stamped all over it. When his dad finally did come home, Alex was setting the table, something he normally had to be nagged to do. His father raised an eyebrow, said, "Hi," then went into his room. No sign of anger.

Alex was putting the water jug on the table when he remembered the black jacket on the couch. He took it to his room and shoved it into his closet, next to the brick and the weight-lifting magazines. His father was finishing the dinner preparations when he emerged. Frozen meals in the microwave tonight. Dead easy. They sat at the table to eat, only speaking to ask for salt or pepper or whatever else was out of reach. Then, out of nowhere, his father asked him what he had planned for the weekend.

Alex froze. Horrible possibilities ran through his mind. His dad had seen the Jockey that day near his shop. Or he'd talked to the school, found out the Jockey was back. Or worse, somehow his dad knew about the sleep rough weekend. Alex was tempted to blurt everything out, say that it had all been the Jockey's idea, that he was too afraid to say no.

He didn't.

No way was he a baby.

So he faked it, took longer to chew, thought about what he should say. Probably it had just been an innocent question. His father wanted to know what he had planned at his mom's house for the weekend, that was all. Then he remembered the phone call from his mother yesterday.

"Alex?" said his father, glass of water poised. "You gonna answer me?"

"Yeah, um, nothing much . . ."

Now was the choice. Tell his dad about the phone call, about the change of plans, or say nothing. He could see the two possibilities before him, like shining beacons. Say that his mom couldn't have him this weekend. That he had to stay home. Easy. There was no way he could sneak out from his father. The Jockey would understand the iron rule he lived under. The sleep rough idea would come down to nothing, and no one could blame him.

"Everything okay, Alex?" asked his dad.

Or lie, and take on the night. His father was still waiting.

All he had to do was speak. To say a few words. Alex went to cut some more of his dinner, only to notice that his hand was shaking. He dropped the knife and fork onto the plate and pushed it away. He was no longer hungry.

"You okay?" said his father. "No problems at Mom's, is there?"

"No, Dad. It's cool . . ."

"It doesn't look cool." His father put his glass down with a snap. "Alex, what is it?"

So gentle was his father's tone that he might as well have reached over and touched him. A great knot grew in Alex's throat. Could he just drop a *hint* about the sleep rough weekend, perhaps? Let his dad figure it out? The old man might even grin and say it's a stupid idea, but amazing just the same. He'd been a boy, too, hadn't he? He'd done crazy things. If you believed half of what old Poppa used to say, then his dad had been a wild little nutcase. You don't forget a whole part of your life that easily.

There was a tiny crack that opened in that moment, a slice that he could put his hand through. Alex could rush in and be embraced . . . Then his father spoke again. Calmly, deceptively quiet.

"Is it Rod?" he asked. "Is he giving you a hard time?"

And the crack snapped shut. So that was it. Yet another reason to find fault with his mom's new husband. Why hadn't he seen it coming? He should have recognized the look on his father's face. The terrible anger, mixed with defeat.

"Dad," he mumbled. "I really don't want to talk about it."

That only served to make his father *more* paranoid that something was up, and that it *had* to be Rod who was at fault.

"He's got nothing to do with your upbringing," he said, voice raising in pitch. "As far as I'm concerned he can stay right out of it . . ."

"Dad, I hardly ever speak to him . . ."

"He's not family." His father was almost shouting.

Alex closed his eyes, his hands clenched into hard balls under the table, his body rigid. The storm wasn't coming, it was here.

"You're my son!" Now he was shouting. "I have a right to know what you're doing on these weekends. *She* didn't want you. She made that perfectly clear. *She* couldn't cope with you. *She* had another life to live with Rod the oh-so-clever lover-boy . . ."

It was a strange feeling watching a grown man go red in the face and have a tantrum. Alex felt quite detached from it all, but also relieved that his dad's temper had led him away from any suspicions. Then a sadness took over, and he stood abruptly, taking his plate to the kitchen. He could hear the Jockey's voice in his head, *"Your daddy got you tied up in frigging knots, man."*

Could feel the snap and twang as they broke away.

"What would your old man know, anyway? Got his head stuck up his arse where all his accounts and sales are . . ."

Sometimes it felt more like a rip than a twang.

"This is gonna be so frigging amazing . . ."

Later, he went into his room and shut the door, waiting until he heard his father go to bed. Then he turned his light off, but he couldn't sleep. Couldn't let his mind rest.

Everything was about to change.

Everything.

THE CITY

THERE COMES A TIME IN EVERY RIGHTLY CONSTRUCTED
BOY'S LIFE WHEN HE HAS A RAGING DESIRE TO GO SOMEWHERE
AND DIG FOR HIDDEN TREASURE.

—MARK TWAIN

CHAPTER NINE

There was nothing wild about the city that Friday afternoon. Alex saw shoppers milling around, teenagers in school uniforms hanging together in groups, office workers rushing from this place to that. Hardly the wilderness the Jockey had promised. Even so, he wasn't disappointed. Just making it this far had been an achievement.

Ever since he'd made the decision to go through with the weekend, he'd had to lie, manipulate the truth, *and* avoid Marta. She was the hardest, of course, because she knew that something was up. Catching the earlier bus to school had kept her off his trail for a while, and walking to Marble Hill shops after school instead of getting the South bus home had also worked. Then he learned that Marta had been away for most of the week, anyway, so he could have saved his energy.

Next challenge was making sure his father and mother didn't

talk to each other during the week. That way his dad wouldn't find out that the Mom weekend wasn't happening.

Normally it wouldn't be so difficult to keep his parents apart, as they basically hated each other, but ever since the tantrum over Rod, his dad had been asking more questions about what went on at his mother's house. "Are you ever alone with Rod? Does he try to tell you what to do? Is he there often? Blah? Blah? Blah?" It took all of Alex's skill to tiptoe his way through the minefield of his father's anger, making up answers that would sound right, but wouldn't get his dad so worked up that he'd call his mom to shout at her. That'd be the end of the plan, because sooner or later they'd figure out that they both thought the other was taking care of him.

Alex said whatever he thought would work, and in the end, the truth got so buried in lies and sham that he had no idea what he really thought about his mom or the fact that he had a stepdad. In fact, he didn't even care. As far as he was concerned, they could all go and play their silly jealous games without him.

By Friday morning Alex felt weary, not excited. Over breakfast his father had asked if he'd packed his bag. "Yeah, I packed. It's in my room." Another lie. They were slipping off his tongue so easily that he even started believing them. He could see the bag sitting on his bed, full of clothes and computer games. But there was no bag because there was nothing to pack. Not for where he was headed.

All he needed were his wits . . .

"Should I call you at Mom's?" his father had asked, just as he was about to leave for school.

"What would you wanna do that for?" he'd snapped back.

It was dangerous to speak to his father this way, and he

waited for the tirade, but to his surprise his father had simply sighed.

"Okay," he'd said. "Take care of yourself."

Try as he might, Alex couldn't get those words out of his head.

Now he was on the bench seat in the mall checking out nothing in particular, rocking out of boredom with his hands in the black jacket's pockets. There was a man nearby with a microphone trying to sell perfume to the passing trade. He wasn't getting very far. It was just another ordinary day in an ordinary city. "Dopey people spending money they didn't have on crap they didn't need." That was what his dad sometimes said when Alex asked him about the shop.

This place was so depressingly familiar. Alex looked over at the Jockey, who was lighting up another cigarette. He had a small book of matches, which he flicked open then snapped shut rhythmically. The Jockey had hardly said a word since they'd met in the mall, just nodded at him as if he was a passing acquaintance, then sat on the seat with his hands in his pockets, looking as if he had somewhere better to be. Alex had followed suit, sitting on the bench and waiting . . . but waiting for what? To be covered in the Jockey's cigarette smoke? To wonder why he had to come carrying nothing at all, not even five cents to his name, yet the Jockey could turn up with his smokes and his matches as if that was all okay?

They'd set rules. They'd worked it out over the week. Come with nothing more than the clothes on your back. No money. Nothing. "Just like them dudes in the frigging book," the Jockey had said. "Only they had a spear, eh?"

Alex had tried to start up a few conversations, but the Jockey had only grunted. Once, he'd stood up in the middle of Alex speaking to walk over to the trash can, spit into it, then return to the seat and sniff. All the bubbling fizz of nerves and excitement that had been with Alex since the final bell had sounded at school that afternoon was dribbling away. He thought he'd try one last time, see if he could get the Jockey to say something.

"Are we gonna . . . you know. . . . Are we gonna actually *do* something?"

The Jockey snorted again, flicking the cigarette butt where it bounced and rolled, narrowly missing a rushing passerby. He stretched his legs out and nodded at the activity in the mall, mumbling, "Some hunting ground, eh?"

Alex looked at him. Was that it? Was that the answer to his question? What did he mean by that? He decided to grunt in agreement, see if he couldn't draw his quiet guide out a bit more.

The Jockey snorted next to him, as if Alex had said something stupid. This was too much. "What?" exploded Alex. "What'd I say?"

"You didn't say nothing," said the Jockey. "Which is quite frigging funny when you look at it. You talk too much when there's nothing to say, and you say nothing when it's time to talk. You're all half-arsed and up bog creek, ain't ya?"

Alex was stunned by the attack. He wanted to retort, to fight back, but he found that he had nothing to say. Could the Jockey be right? Was he that much of an empty air bag? What was the phrase he'd once heard his father use? "All piss and wind." He sat up straighter, angry, saying, "Well, what about you?"

"What about me?" snorted the Jockey.

"You're all . . . you know. . . . The big guy who's gonna teach me and stuff. . . . And you haven't done anything."

The Jockey shook his head slowly. "Whatya want? A blackboard? Look at ya. Gonna sleep out for the night. Gonna hold my hand and follow me around . . ."

His words stung and Alex looked away. Why the attack? Did the Jockey have second thoughts? Was he trying to get out of the weekend?

"Now what are ya doing?" sighed the Jockey.

Alex shrugged.

The Jockey slapped him playfully across the back of the head. "Geez, you're a funny little nutcase, ain't ya?" he said. "You frigging awake, yet?" He waved his arm about the mall. "This is your hunting ground, eh? Your territory. You wanna earn respect, you earn it here. But *you* do it. Not me."

Alex wanted to ask how, but knew what sort of a response this would bring. Instead he looked out at his hunting ground, the mall, taking in every detail: the people going home, lining up for buses, grabbing last minute purchases from the late-night shops. What did he hunt for in this place? His stomach started to growl, and he smiled. Food would be a good idea. Several groups of office workers sat around steel tables outside a nearby pub, shouting and laughing. Alex could smell their perfume and aftershave, mixed with cigarettes and beer. But it was the aroma of hot French fries that nearly sent him crashing from his seat. It was driving him crazy.

He reached instinctively for his wallet, then stopped. It wasn't there. He was so used to buying food or going to the kitchen whenever he was hungry. Now what did he do? No one had ever taught him how to deal with a situation like this. The Jockey was right. He *was* soft. Conditioned for years to "Go ask a policeman," or "Speak to a responsible adult" if anything scary ever happened.

"Hungry, eh?" asked the Jockey.

Alex turned to him and nodded. "You bet," he said.

"Then go get some food."

He looked around at the mall again, at the crowds of blank, anonymous faces, then shook his head. "What do I do?" he said, frustration growing. "I can't figure it out . . ."

"I can't figure it out," mimicked the Jockey, putting on a baby voice. "First sign of trouble and you whine like a girl. Is that what you are? A girl?"

"Shut up," snapped Alex.

"Do you think I wet my pants inside Barlow Road every time something went wrong?" said the Jockey. "Do ya?"

Alex shook his head. "It's easy for you," he said. "You're like . . . you know . . . tough and that. You know how to fight . . ."

The Jockey laughed. "Fight," he said, shaking his head. "You wanted to know what it was like inside? I'll tell ya. You drive into the place in an ordinary car, right? Everything ordinary. Just a frigging station wagon. Everyone's ordinary around you, too. No uniforms or nightsticks or guns. Got a caseworker and she's ordinary, too. Dresses in normal clothes, because this is just a frigging vacation camp, right? They process you, show you your room, then you're on your own. And now they're watching you, Alex."

"Who?" he asked.

"Who do you frigging think? The other inmates. You're in the frigging jungle and real quick you gotta find out the rules. How do you survive in this place? What do you get away with? Are you gonna be a hunter? Or are you there to be hunted? First day, little Alex. Because the other bastards, they surround ya, check ya out. 'What's ya name?' 'What ya in for?' 'Did ya murder someone?' They eye you, see if you're stronger than them or if you're weaker. And it ain't just your muscles they're watching.

You think that might be scary, little bro? You frigging betcha it is. This was one freaky place. But did I wet my pants and cry and say, 'I don't know what to do'? Of course not. I wasn't going to let them turn me into their frigging bunny. And do ya think I started swinging punches? Of course not. I wasn't gonna end up doing extra time, neither. I just looked 'em fair in the eye and bulked up. Told them I'd done a copper in. Hit him with a bat. Gave them something to think about. I *impressed* them, little Alex. And I didn't have to hurt no one to do it."

The Jockey was almost shouting by this stage, and Alex leaned away from him a little, frightened by the intensity in his eyes. The Jockey regarded him for a moment, then said, "Well, go on! Get us something to eat. I'm hungry."

Alex glared at him, then stood. He'd prove that he wasn't a crybaby. He'd said yes to the idea of the weekend, hadn't he? He'd lied to get here. What scared little kid would do that? He paced out into the mall, the hunter, no spear in his hand, no idea in his head. As his stomach growled, the reality of the situation hit home. How was he going to do it? He couldn't go into a shop and ask for food, they'd just kick him out. And he didn't want to steal any, that was too risky. There was no way he was going to rummage through the trash for scraps. They weren't that desperate.

The Jockey had told him this was his hunting ground, but what did that mean? That he knew all the animals, all the dangers? Still didn't tell him where the food was. Alex looked around. He could see some very familiar "animals." Teenage kids eating fries next to the fountain, throwing the small ones at one another for fun. They were tough, and you only approached them with caution. A man in his mid-twenties eating a hot dog, leaning forward so the sauce didn't drip. He was unpredictable. He might turn and attack at the slightest provocation. A chunk of the man's hot dog fell onto the ground, and he quickly kicked the meat under his seat.

Alex cursed him beneath his breath.

There was a woman with small children handing out potato chips from a bag, and Alex knew not to go near her. She'd be frightened, run away, or call the authorities. Then he spotted a businessman in a suit with a bag of hot fries. He looked uncomfortable, holding the fries away from his clothes, picking unenthusiastically at them. He'd probably grabbed them on a whim, and he seemed more concerned about keeping his hands and clothes clean than eating. Alex saw an opportunity.

He went into the nearest deli and grabbed some paper napkins from the dispenser on the counter, taking them over to the businessman.

"Here," he said, holding out the paper napkins.

The businessman looked at him with a slightly confused expression on his face.

"You looked like you might need these," said Alex.

"Thanks," said the man, taking the paper napkins. He clearly wanted to wipe his hands, but he was still holding the fries and could only make clumsy attempts. Eventually he held the fries up to Alex, saying, "Would you?"

Alex took them. The man wiped his hands free of the fat and oil, then looked up at Alex and waved casually at the bag. "Keep them," he said.

"Thanks," said Alex, returning to the Jockey with the half full bag of fries. "See," he said, holding up the prize. "I got some food." If he'd been looking for praise, he received very little. "Mm," said his companion, taking more than his fair share. Even the Jockey's pigging of the fries didn't dent Alex's feeling of triumph. Nothing anyone had ever said to him, no praise from a teacher, no pat on the back from a parent, could even come close to how good it felt to get that food. This *was* his wilderness. He knew how to read it, how to go in and take what he needed. It had been so cool, figuring out who he could approach and who he couldn't. He was smart—street-smart, even—and he'd get through this sleep rough night for sure. The fries vanished in the space of a few seconds, and Alex threw the empty bag into the trash.

"Okay," said the Jockey, wiping his greasy hands on his jeans. "Time for some real hunting." He stood and surveyed the mall, a slow smile coming to his face. Sitting two seats away was a boy, about twelve or thirteen, just watching the action around him. The kid was alone, and the Jockey walked right up to him, standing almost on his toes, talking in a low voice that Alex couldn't hear. The kid shook his head a few times, looking around nervously, but the Jockey always seemed able to snap his attention back to him. Alex watched the kid eventually reach into his pocket and pull out a five-dollar bill, which he dropped into the Jockey's hand.

With a wink at Alex, the Jockey sauntered into a take-out restaurant, but Alex was still watching the victim. The kid hung his head for a moment, his face red and withdrawn. Was he angry or embarrassed? Alex wanted to say something to him, ask if he was okay perhaps, but the kid stood abruptly and walked away, tears welling in his eyes. He quickly vanished into the crowd. Still Alex watched for him.

"Want some?"

The Jockey had returned with a big bag of fries and a soft drink. He held the plunder out, but Alex shook his head. He wasn't hungry anymore. His companion continued to eat noisily, obviously enjoying the fact that his haul had been much bigger than Alex's. After a few minutes, he spoke with a mouthful of food.

"Man, you gotta think big, you know? We'd starve if all we had was you hunting for us . . ."

Alex shrugged his shoulders. Suddenly this wasn't such an exciting game anymore. He contemplated calling it quits, going home and admitting his deception to his father when the Jockey put his arm around his shoulders.

"You get used to it. Being hard, I mean. The brothers taught me that."

"Brothers?" asked Alex.

"Inside Barlow Road. The brothers. They were the ones, you know, they taught me that you gotta be hard. Otherwise, you're just a pussy like that kid, handing over your money without a fight."

Alex turned to the Jockey. So he'd had brothers inside Barlow Road, and now he was being a big brother himself, taking care of the little "Grub." Shouting at him, pushing him into doing things he'd never done before. Is that what a big brother did? Were they sometimes angry? Sometimes cruel? Sometimes very, very frightening . . . ? Alex had no way of knowing. He figured that whatever a big brother was, the one thing he *had* to do was stick by his little brother. Blood ties weren't made to be broken. But he and the Jockey had no such ties. All they'd done was read books together and talk about a plan . . .

"Why do you wanna do this?" asked Alex, a cold knot of suspicion growing in him. "You know . . . teach me to be a man and stuff?"

"I told ya already," said the Jockey, masking a brief flash of anger. Alex tensed instinctively, but the Jockey smiled and punched him playfully on the upper arm. "Look at ya," he said. "You're a little toughie. You know that? A little toughie. You've almost stepped over the line, my little bro. You've had your first hunt, and there's plenty more to come. I can see you're different already. There ain't nothing ordinary about you no more. Come on, we got work to do."

He stood, shaking his legs, then moved off quickly. Alex stared at him for a moment, the blurred colors of the passing shoppers flashing in the corner of his eye. Had he changed already? He stepped out into the middle of the throng and a man stopped short to avoid a collision. "Sorry," the man muttered, then stepped around him. Alex smiled. Maybe he had. That man had stopped for him. Respected *him*!

He ran after the Jockey, into the dark, the late-night shoppers thinning out with each block. He *did* feel different. It was almost as if the passing scenery belonged to another world. These weren't people passing him, they were opportunities. And these weren't streets he was on, they were places of danger if you didn't know what to look out for. Alex was beginning to see the hidden signs, the stuff going on that ordinary people would not notice.

Maybe the Jockey was right. Maybe all he had to do was toughen up a little. He watched the Jockey weave his way through the pedestrians, his arms bulky with muscle, his gait strong and sure. Without even being aware of it, Alex started to copy him. They had "work" to do, and judging by the five-dollar kid, it'd be hard work indeed. Alex prepared himself, told himself it had to be done. There was no way that anyone would call him a wimp or a wuss. Not anymore.

He was a hunter.

Chapter TEN

They were well away from the city center now, into the darker streets where the traffic was sparse and irregular, where the shopfronts were cold and uninteresting. They were heading down their own private pathway, long and dark, with no light at the end. All around were people going about their business. Getting out of cars, going into restaurants, talking on mobile phones, waiting for taxis. The Jockey weaved past them as if they weren't even there. He had a destination in mind.

The air was growing colder now that the sun had gone completely. Alex couldn't help thinking that he was leaving something behind with each step that he took. It was more than just the old Alex, the dribbly kid who thought it was cool to crack jokes at his own dunking. He was leaving behind the world where he knew how the rules worked, knew the right thing and the wrong thing because they'd been drilled into him since Marta was pushing him over in her front yard. He was leaving behind a world where it was supposedly safe to sit on a seat in the middle of the mall and not be robbed or harassed.

The Jockey had shown him how different things really were. Could he take this new path? He thought about that kid in the mall, the look on his face. In one short minute, he'd changed from a normal dude in the city, hanging back, relaxed, into . . . What? A victim?

Alex caught up with the Jockey, asking, "What did you say to that kid back there?"

The Jockey sniffed, then said, "You felt sorry for him, didn't ya?"

"No," lied Alex. "Who cares about him?"

The Jockey snorted. "You did."

"I didn't," insisted Alex.

The Jockey stopped and grabbed him by his jacket, gripping him tight.

"You think carefully about what you frigging say, little Alex. Remember what I told ya? When you open your mouth, make sure it means something. So you think long, slow, and frigging hard about your answer."

The Jockey released his grip and smiled. Alex took a step backward, unruffling his jacket.

"You're thinking scared now, ain't ya?" said his guide and teacher. "Thinking I'm gonna lose my nut if you say the wrong thing, eh? I'm not your daddy, Alex. Only losers think like that. You a loser?"

"No," said Alex.

"Then you tell me true. Did you feel sorry for that kid?"

Alex didn't want to tell the truth. It would reveal that he was still soft, still clinging to the old world. He wanted to be strong, to convince, to impress.

The Jockey continued to smile, but there was a hint behind the expression, a mocking leer that unsettled Alex. This was a test, like one of those moral or ethical questions that hurt his brain in school. Only this time the answer wasn't rhetorical, wasn't mindless bull spouted to sound right. Alex knew that the Jockey was opening a door for him. What had he said earlier? *"You've almost stepped over the line."*

Alex felt his jaw clench with tension, then he spoke in his most assertive voice, "I told ya!" Almost shouting. "He don't mean nothing to me. So I don't feel sorry for him. He was just five dollars. That's all."

His teacher's face was impassive. Alex's heart raced, but the words had sounded right as they came out. He almost believed it himself. . . . He *did* believe it. There was an unbearable pause, then the Jockey smiled and pulled a chocolate bar from his pocket and tossed it casually to Alex.

"Saved this for ya," he said, then looked away.

Alex unwrapped the chocolate bar and began devouring it, surprised at how hungry he still was. He'd finished it all before he realized he hadn't offered the Jockey any. Not that his teacher seemed to mind. He was still surveying the "wilderness" around them, a look of disdain on his face.

The Jockey lit up another cigarette, opening and closing the flap on the book of matches with one hand, holding his cigarette in the cup of the other. "I hate this frigging place," he muttered. He turned to Alex. "You ever really hated something? Huh? I mean, *really* frigging hated it? I tell ya, I hate this place." He blew a plume of smoke into the air and it vanished into the night. "All the stuck-up snobs and the know-it-alls and the do-gooders that run the whole, freaking show. They're at ya all the time. 'Be polite.' 'Be nice.' 'Be good.' Be a nobody. Can you see it, little Alex? Can you see how this place works?" His gaze wandered again, scanning the area around them. "See that guy over there . . . ?" The Jockey gestured toward a man standing at a taxi with his wallet out, paying the fare. "His mind's on a whole heap of stuff. What he's gonna have for dinner. What his wife's gonna yell at him for. But the thing his mind isn't on is that frigging wallet, eh? That's what you gotta watch out for, little bro. Opportunities. They're all around you. Easy money, if you know how to take it. Go in there and take what you frigging can. That's the right thing to do. You think the world works any other way? Man, look at those business guys, earning millions of bucks for being total screwups." He flicked his cigarette butt away, then lit a match, holding it in his hand. "Life is dangerous, Alex." The match burned down to his fingers, but he didn't flinch. Just watched it sear his skin. Then he threw it to the ground. "So, that guy over there? I watch him, and I wait. If there's an opening . . . I grab it."

Alex looked at the man as he closed his wallet and walked into a restaurant. He seemed big, muscular. No way he'd try to snatch that guy's wallet.

"People are careful with their money," said Alex.

The Jockey nodded. "Yeah, but not always. You see, that's the kind of information you get in a place like Barlow. Man, those guys, they knew so much. I mean, I learned how to get into all sorts of makes of cars, how to start them, how to get into houses, even the ones with grilles on the windows. I learned so much, little Alex."

"Will you teach me?" he asked, excited by the knowledge, though not sure if he'd ever use it.

"You're a keen little bugger, ain't ya," said the Jockey.

He started walking again, and Alex stepped in beside him. This was more like it, the Jockey was doing what he promised— teaching. He felt powerful again, able to cut through the crowds and the streets and anything associated with an "ordinary" life. He *knew* how the world worked now.

They were heading for a major road that ran around the outskirts of the city. Alex wondered what lay beyond, even wondered if it was safe now to ask. Coming to a traffic crossing, they stopped to wait for the green light. Hunters have to obey some laws.

Alex took a deep breath, then asked, "Where *are* we headed?"

"To meet the dead people," said the Jockey.

"Dead people? Really?"

"Yeah. Why? You scared?"

"No," lied Alex.

"You'll like this place," said the Jockey. "You won't find posh pussies in suits here. No easy marks for ya."

The lights were taking forever to change, and the Jockey waited impatiently, changing his weight from foot to foot.

"Why'd you come back from Queensland, anyway?" asked Alex.

The Jockey didn't turn or look at him, just stared ahead at the red light. "My mom wanted to come home," he said. "Queensland sucked, anyway. Everyone was too happy. I'd rather be in a place where people think life is crap. Better opportunities there. Besides, I had some unfinished business with you."

The lights changed, and the Jockey set off across the street before Alex had a chance to follow up on that last comment. He had to run to keep up, and his heart was racing but not from the exercise. Why did the Jockey do that? Throw in stuff about "unfinished business," just when he thought they were getting along fine? They kept up a rapid pace until they came to a busy road. There was no crossing, so the Jockey checked the flow of the traffic, then ran across to the middle. Alex picked his own gap and gave chase. He perched precariously next to the Jockey on a narrow concrete divider. The traffic screamed past them, blowing dusty wind into their faces.

"You wanna play chicken?" shouted the Jockey.

"How's that?" asked Alex.

"Chicken. You gotta run when I say so. If you don't, you're a chicken."

"And if I do?"

"Tough guy." The Jockey grinned.

Alex looked at the traffic, it was treacherously fast. Every now and then there were small gaps in the flow that a fast runner could get through. Okay, if the Jockey wanted to play, then he'd play. "Let's go for it," he said, and the older boy grinned at him, looking up to the oncoming traffic.

"Get ready . . ."

Alex crouched, watching the traffic.

"Go!" shouted the Jockey.

Was he kidding? There was no gap in the traffic. It would have been certain death if he'd run across.

"Chicken!" The Jockey laughed. "Little chicken . . ."

"No way could I cross," shouted Alex. "You knew that."

"Chicken . . ."

"Give me another try."

The Jockey called him "chicken" a few more times, then eventually agreed to another turn. He watched the traffic. A large gap was approaching, but the Jockey stayed mute. Alex could see a smaller, more dangerous gap in the traffic coming after, and he tensed, the cars seeming to have picked up speed. Sure enough, as soon as the small gap was just about on him, the Jockey shouted, "Go!"

This time Alex was ready for it and hurtled himself across the road, his heart pounding, his mouth sick with the taste of adrenaline. A car blasted its horn at him, and he skipped in the air, expecting to be knocked sideways. Instead he reached the other side of the road and tripped on the sewer drain, landing face-first on the sidewalk.

After a pause, he heard the Jockey laughing above him, and he turned, grinning, saying, "I did it."

"Yeah, little tough guy. You did it," said the Jockey, looking down at him with an expression that was almost affectionate. Then it suddenly hardened, and the Jockey looked past Alex, down the road. "Crap," he muttered, then "Run!"

He was gone, and Alex scrambled to his feet, wondering what had set him off like that. He shot a quick glance down the road and saw a police car, pulled over hastily, blocking the traffic. Two cops were emerging from the car, looking directly at Alex. They'd obviously seen the game of chicken.

He turned and ran, shouting for the Jockey to slow down, but of course there was no way he'd do that, so Alex put in his longest strides. There were mostly shops along this road. Their only hope was to turn down a side street and make it difficult to catch them so that the cops would give up the chase. After all, it wasn't as if they'd been seen robbing a bank.

They were nearing a small lane, and Alex knew instinctively that the Jockey would make it his exit. He felt proud of himself when his guide did make a quick turn right, only a few paces ahead by now. His pride, however, rapidly dissolved when he turned into the darkened exit to see no sign of the Jockey anywhere.

Alex swore loudly and was answered by a whispering voice, "Shut up and get in here." "Here" was a narrow gap between two large buildings, a dank, dark crack that he barely managed to squeeze into. He'd just hidden the last of himself when he heard the sound of feet running into the lane. The police went past their hiding spot, and Alex strained to hear them, until they were only a distant noise.

"What are they doing?" hissed the Jockey.

"How the hell would I know?" whispered Alex. "My nose is squashed against a brick."

The Jockey started giggling beside him, releasing the tension from the chase, and Alex laughed with him. It was crazy making so much noise, and they pinched each other to stem their humor.

"Ouch! Not so frigging hard," whispered the Jockey.

"Ssh!"

The cops were returning, their flashlights shining narrow beams of light across the lane. They stopped near their hiding spot, silent, light searching the darkest of places. Alex was certain that they'd be found now. He felt like a little kid in a game of hide-and-seek, wanting to squeal out, "Here I am!"—anything to un-bottle the tension and excitement. A quick shaft of light flashed across his face, then all was dark again. They listened as the cops left the lane, then Alex started shuffling from their hiding spot when the Jockey grabbed him by the arm.

"Stay here," he hissed.

Alex froze. Of course, the cops could be waiting for them just around the corner. He cursed himself for being so stupid.

They waited for five minutes, then cautiously wriggled from their hiding spot, making their way farther down into the darkness of the lane. It wasn't until they were several minutes away that they allowed themselves to explode with laughter, shouting at each other, "Did you see that copper . . . ?" and "Man, I thought I'd . . ." and "That was so frigging close . . ."

Eventually they sat on the curb of a lonely little street. Alex said, "What would those coppers have done with us, anyway? Drive us home or something?"

The Jockey gave him a superior look and shook his head.

"What?" said Alex.

"You don't know nothing, do ya?" he said. "Drive us frigging home. What then? Tell us a good-night story and tuck us in? Jeezus, Alex. Grow up, man. I'm on frigging probation, you jerk. You know what that means?"

The smile that had frozen on Alex's face now faded into a frown. He shook his head, not sure about what "probation" might mean, but certain he was going to be told, anyway.

"Release on recognizance," spat the Jockey. "Under probation for twelve frigging months. You think that doing time in Barlow is the end of it? What a joke. They got you by the balls for years, man. I got conditions, you get it? Good behavior and all that. I gotta be home every night. No alcohol, no mixing with anyone of a criminal element, and it's my mom who'll pay if I break the bond. Not to mention they'll probably put me in foster care or back in Barlow. So no, little Alex, they ain't gonna just drive us frigging home."

He felt so stupid for not knowing what was now obvious. Of course they were going to keep a check on the Jockey, make sure he didn't stray again.

"That means," said Alex, suddenly realizing what was right before his nose, "you're really risking a lot doing this sleep rough weekend, then."

The Jockey clapped his hands slowly, saying, "You're a little genius when you put your mind to it."

Alex blushed, stung yet again by the Jockey's sarcasm. He wanted to say something to him, a thank-you, perhaps. Instead he gobbed up a huge spitball in his mouth and let fly with it, satisfied that it sailed all the way to the middle of the road. The Jockey laughed.

"So, what about your dad, then?" said Alex.

"What about him?" muttered the Jockey.

"Is he, like, supposed to make sure you're in bed and all that? I mean, how come he don't belt you and stuff for running wild on the weekend?"

The Jockey was shaking his head again, an annoying habit that Alex knew he wouldn't comment on. "My dad?" he said. "My old man wouldn't know me if he fell over me. You're such a little jerk at times."

Alex turned away from the Jockey. Why did he have to be so damned hard to talk to? Why put him down and make him feel so small?

"The last time I seen my dad was when I was born," said the Jockey bitterly. "And I don't frigging remember it. My mom says they had to drag him into the hospital room when she was having me. Did not wanna be there. Stood in the corner the whole time looking like he was gonna faint. My mom screamed and yelled at him until I popped out. Then the nurse got me and wrapped me up in a blanket and took me over to him. 'This is your son,' she said to him. And he leans over, like, looks at me and says, 'Funny-looking little bugger, isn't he.' Then he just ups and walks out of the room. Mom never heard from him again."

The Jockey started laughing, a fake, forced sound. He slapped Alex on the back, said, "Funny story, eh?"

Alex shook his head. No, it wasn't funny.

Now the Jockey moved closer. "What's the matter, little Alex?"

he cooed in Alex's ear. "Disappointed that my daddy's as big a dick as yours?" He had a knowing look on his face, as if he was waiting for something. An argument, perhaps? Words from Alex in defense of his father?

When nothing came, he smiled. Nodded his head.

"This is where the fun begins," he said. He drew an imaginary line across the road with his boot. "Coming?"

Then he turned and walked down the street.

Alex stayed where he was and shook his legs. He watched the Jockey depart, and for a brief moment, he contemplated turning in the opposite direction.

Instead he crossed over the boot-rubber mark on the road and followed. Into the night. Into the unknown.

CHAPTER ELEVEN

They were standing under a long, wide, and high wall that flanked the sidewalk, spreading out for a hundred yards either side. It had taken almost half an hour to walk here, and neither of them had spoken to each other the whole time. The quiet had allowed Alex to calm down, to think and to eventually realize that he wanted to stay in the game, as dangerous as it was gradually becoming. He felt that he owed it at least to the Jockey, who was sacrificing a lot by being out at night.

"What's over here?" asked Alex, looking up at the wall.

"Cemetery," said the Jockey.

"Really?" He hoped the Jockey hadn't heard the note of fear in his voice.

"I come here sometimes," said the Jockey. "Get myself an intellectual conversation . . ." He started laughing at his own joke, a harsh, spiteful sound. "This is where we're gonna meet the dead people. There's, like, spirits over this wall. Really. I seen them."

"Bull," said Alex.

"It's frigging true. There's this one ghost, he's like, just a voice or something. Runs his creepy, cold fingers over your scalp. . . ."

Alex could feel the icy probes in his hair and shuddered a little. He thrust his hands into his jacket pocket and smiled knowingly, saying, "Gee, I'm real scared."

"You will be," said the Jockey ominously. He jumped up, just managing to get a grip on the top of the wall, heaving and kicking and pulling himself to the top. "Come on," he said, once he'd balanced on his perch. Then he jumped over and was gone.

It took Alex several attempts before he, too, could get a grip on the top of the wall. By the time he'd scrambled over, there was no sign of the Jockey on the other side. It was dark here, cut off from the streetlights, and Alex could make out vague shapes ahead that looked like trees. He called out, "Hey," a few times, but there was no answer. There didn't seem to be anywhere else to go but the trees, so he set off in that direction. He had to rely on feeling the ground slowly with his feet, his arms outstretched, stumbling now and then on the uneven and patchy terrain. Step by step, calling out the Jockey's name. Still no answer.

Eventually he reached the trees, and it seemed darker here, with visibility down to a few feet. There was a pinprick of light ahead, through the foliage, orange and flickering, probably a fire of some sort. He sped up toward it, until he grazed the top of his head on a low branch and saw stars. Swearing loudly, Alex leaned against the tree and rubbed his head. This was *not* fun! He was about twenty or thirty yards into the clump of trees by now, and he moved off slowly, once again feeling cautiously with his feet on the treacherous ground. After only a few more steps, the ground dropped away completely beneath him.

"Now what?" Alex sighed.

"Sit down," hissed a harsh voice.

Alex froze. A horrid icy fear tingled through his scalp and almost sent him running. Had that been a man's voice? Or was it . . . ? He looked around, but the darkness was so complete that any one of the shadowy, looming shapes around him could be the owner of the voice, if in fact he had a body.

"What are you doing here, sonny?" asked the voice.

"Looking for my friend . . ."

"He ain't here, unless he died."

Alex backed away from the direction of the voice, weighing his options up in his mind. If he ran, he was likely to hit a tree again. He could try hiding in the foliage, but whoever, or whatever, was near him seemed to have better eyesight in the dark than he did.

"This is where the spirits play, boy," sneered the voice.

It was loud, hissing in his ear. He could feel the fine spray of it. Alex jumped away instinctively, cracking his shoulder into a branch. He cried out in pain.

There was a small chuckle. "This is where the dead do their dirty work. Settle old scores with the living." The voice laughed again, and Alex felt a revulsion rise in his throat.

"Only way out is to pay a price. What are you prepared to give?"

"Nothing," said Alex, backing away slowly.

"Nothing? What's that you're wearing?"

"My clothes. Why?"

"I know they're your clothes, you idiot. Is that a jacket?"

Alex instinctively pulled his black denim jacket tighter around his body. He was convinced now that it was a man speaking and not a ghost. This certainty came as no comfort, however, because a man would have arms and muscles and the will to do him some real harm.

"I like the look of that jacket. I reckon I'll have it . . ."

"No way!" shouted Alex.

"Listen to me," hissed the man. "You ain't used to this light, I am. You ain't armed, but I am. So give me the jacket and no one's gonna get hurt."

A hard hand gripped Alex on the arm, and he could smell his enemy—musty sweat and damp tobacco. He swung his fist around, but all he hit was fresh air. The man laughed, whispering in Alex's ear, "You can't hit a ghost." Alex turned quickly, kicking out at the voice, but once again he missed completely. He told himself that this was not a ghost. They don't smell so bad, for a start. The guy was fast, that was all. And he could see better in the dark. Then he remembered the crack about being armed. Something cold touched him on the cheek. Alex yelled, lashing out with both arms. Once again he hit nothing.

"You're gonna fall over if you keep that up." The man laughed.

"Shut up," said Alex. "My friend will be here soon. He's tough, he'll get you . . ."

"Your friend's left you for dead," hissed the voice.

Alex felt a clip over his ear, and he shouted, "Hey!"

"You gonna give me that jacket? Or do I have to rip it off ya?"

This was hopeless. The man had a total advantage over him. He'd have to hand over the jacket. As he pulled it free, Alex wondered what the hell had happened to his so-called big brother. Fat lot of good he was. He dropped the jacket to the ground and felt a cold wind blow through his T-shirt. Now he felt naked, alone. Anything could come for him here, rip away his flesh, his bones, tear right through him and he wouldn't even see it coming. His only protection had been the Jockey, and now he'd vanished into the night. Even so, Alex thought he could still use him to his advantage. "You'd better be a good runner, Mister," he said.

"And why's that?" came the voice, behind him this time.

"Because my friend . . . my big brother is here, too. He gave me that jacket, so he's gonna be real angry when he finds you took it from me. And he can fight. He's been in prison."

"Whoo, I'm scared," said the man, now in front.

Alex reached down to touch his jacket, but it was gone. He stood, wanting to scream with rage. If only he could see this guy, then he'd be able to kick him or something.

"Every man for himself here." The thief laughed. "Now hand over your pants."

Was he kidding? Hand over his pants? Then what? A hard knot of defiance hit Alex in the gut. No way would he be handing over anything more. It was more than enough that he gave away the jacket. He didn't wait for the ghostly thief to come at him again. Without a care for trees or ditches or personal safety, he ran. Blindly. Bashing his shin against unknown objects that took his breath away with their sharp attack on bone. Landing awkwardly on rocks and roots, rolling his ankle this way and that, registering the pain but putting it aside because the thought of what this man might do to him if he caught up was far stronger than a momentary burning in his joints.

Did he have a knife? Or a gun, perhaps? Would he hear the crack of it flaring? Or would he fall in pain before he heard the gunshot? Crazy thoughts scrambled his mind as he zigzagged through the trees. The pinprick of light was stronger now, and away to his right. It made perfect sense to head for that flickering glow. It spoke of civilization, friends, warmth, safety. Turning sharply, and aware of a noise behind him that seemed to follow his moves, Alex headed for the light. He had a vague sense that the ditch, or the gaping hole he'd encountered earlier, should logically be before him, but what could he do? Maybe he wouldn't fall far? Maybe he'd be able to jump across? Maybe . . .

He fell.

It wasn't a long drop, but it was long enough to knock the wind out of him and leave him moaning on some hard, stony ground. Probably a creek bed by the feel of it. Rising slowly to his knees, he was about to stand when an almighty crash sounded in the bush above him and a dead weight landed on his back. For the second time that night, Alex had the wind knocked out of him. He lay with tears streaming out of his eyes and a burning sensation in his back. Lay with his face pushed into a sharp stone, the sound of laughter in his ear.

"Oh, mate . . ." came the voice above him. "Oh . . . that was the . . . the funniest thing I ever seen."

The Jockey was back.

Alex rolled around, pushing his guide off him. "Where the hell have you been?" he yelled, furious.

"Watching you." The Jockey laughed.

"That guy coulda killed me . . ."

"He woulda stripped you naked first," said the Jockey, standing and brushing his pant legs.

There was a bit more light around, and Alex could see that they were near the edge of the trees now. He clambered up the creek side, followed by the Jockey. The campfire was ahead, about a hundred yards away.

"That was so stupid," he yelled. "You're supposed to be my big brother, and you let him rob me!"

"*I* let him rob you?" said the Jockey, joining him. "That's kinda funny, because it looked to me like *you* let him rob you. I thought you was a toughie. But as soon as some jerk comes at you, you're dropping everything."

"Shut up," snapped Alex, heading for the campfire.

"Oh, please," said the Jockey, putting on a pleading voice. "Do you want my shirt? What about my undies? I'll give you anything, just don't hurt me . . ."

"He said he was armed," snapped Alex. "He was strong. And I couldn't see . . ."

"So?" said the Jockey. "Why didn't you pick up a rock or something? You can't just give up! Man, this is still kiddie-land compared to where we're going. You gonna give away your clothes to every bogeyman you meet? You'll freeze."

Alex didn't answer. The night air seemed to be listening to the Jockey's words. It whipped up cold fingers that reached under Alex's T-shirt and made him shiver. He wrapped his arms around himself, cursing the man in the night who had his jacket. He'd probably sell it for a few dollars, then go buy booze or something. It had been so stupid to give it away. The Jockey was right. He should have fought harder or run earlier.

They headed for the firelight, and Alex listened as they walked. He could hear his footsteps, and the Jockey's, but what was that other sound? Were they being followed? There was something else, too. Something he couldn't put his finger on. It was the air, or the breeze, it just didn't feel right. The campfire was close now, and they could see five people in a clearing huddled around a burning pile of branches. An old man lay dozing against a huge baby carriage with his profile to Alex. He was dressed in a tattered suit, and his head lolled against his chest. A young man and woman were next to him, wrapped in a thin blanket, their legs curled up against the cold. Two younger men in jeans and checked shirts sat on a tree log opposite the old man, leaning forward into the fire for warmth. This strange little group was framed by a line of headstones, some high, some worn down by time, that ran in a long row behind them.

Here they were, the "dead people," the real inhabitants of the cemetery.

The four awake members of the party looked up at them as they emerged from the trees, seemingly disinterested in their arrival. Alex and the Jockey squatted a respectful distance from the fire, nodding their heads at their hosts, who completely ignored them. Even from this distance they could feel the pale warmth from the fire. Alex leaned closer to the flame, allowing himself to soak up the small comfort it offered. A voice spoke beside him, deep and gravelly.

"You look like you've seen a ghostie, son." It was the sleeping old man, looking up from his resting place, his eyes now open.

"Na," said Alex, trying to sound tough. "I just ran into some old jerk back there who tried to rob me of my . . . clothes." He didn't admit that he'd actually lost his jacket, although the Jockey's snort beside him probably gave that away.

"You sure it was a living being?" said the old man, a dead-straight look on his face.

"Yeah . . ."

"You touch him?"

"Yes," lied Alex.

"That's the thing about ghosties," said the old man, looking at the trees from where Alex and the Jockey had emerged. "They's always after your clothes. I call them the shivering spirits.

They're always cold, you see, on account of they got no bodies, and their souls is rotting in hell. A ghost without a soul can't get warm."

"Yeah, sure . . ."

"Feeling cold, son?"

A small shiver ran up Alex's spine. "Just shut up now, okay?" he said.

The two young men in the checked shirts looked up from the fire. Up until now they'd been ignoring the conversation. "Who you telling to shut up?" said the younger of them.

"Sorry," said Alex.

"Don't you come here disrespecting old Alfie . . ."

The Jockey stood beside Alex. "Come on," he said.

Alex stood, too. The old man looked up at him and smiled, a wicked twinkle in his eyes. "I only tell what I see, son," he said. "I only tell the truth . . ."

Alex wanted to shout at him to leave him alone, but the Jockey tugged at his T-shirt, nodding at the younger of the two men who'd risen to his feet, an aggressive look on his face. His mate joined him, prodding the man under the blanket who also stood. They looked toward the boys, anger creasing their hard faces. Alex backed up a few steps, wondering if the Jockey would fight or do the sensible thing and run. The younger man, the natural leader of the group, stooped to pick up a sturdy branch, and his mates followed suit. They weighed their clubs in their hands, waiting for some kind of signal.

"What do we do now?" whispered Alex.

Before the Jockey had a chance to answer, the lead man shouted, "Get the hell out of here!" and the pack ran at them, weapons raised in the air.

CHAPTER TWELVE

A powerful force wrenched Alex by his T-shirt, pulling him backward as the first of the attackers approached. He flinched, expecting a blow to the head or body, but nothing came. The first man ran past him, brushing his shoulder slightly on the way through. Then the second came, missing him completely, and the third followed his comrades. All passed without a second's hesitation.

"Come on," whispered the Jockey in his ear. "This should be interesting."

The force on his T-shirt was released, and he turned to see his "big brother" running back into the woods. "Not again," groaned Alex, then he followed. The three men ahead weaved in and out of the foliage, hugging close to the edge of the trees where the light was better. The Jockey was just behind them. Alex tried to see who they were chasing, catching sight of a dark figure flashing through the gaps in the tree trunks. Each glimpse that he caught seemed to contradict itself. Sometimes the figure appeared large and menacing, other times thin and callow. What were they chasing? A mirage? A shivering ghost? Whoever it was, Alex had the feeling he'd met him before in the woods.

After a minute or two of the hunt, a loud shout erupted ahead, and the group of pursuers came to a halt, milling around someone on the ground. He caught up with the Jockey, who was standing back from the pack, putting his arm out to stop Alex from going any closer to the drama.

"Just wait and watch, little bro," he hissed.

Alex could now see that the three fireside dwellers had surrounded an older man on the ground. He was dressed in shabby sweatpants and a stained Windbreaker, each bearing a myriad of holes. His hands were covered in dirt, and he sat now on his backside shielding himself from any blows that might come his way. The men held their branches at the ready, but none hit him. Could this be the thief in the night who had stolen his jacket?

"We told ya, didn't we?" shouted the leader of the pack. "Don't come back . . ."

"I wasn't. Honest. I was after the lads . . ."

The men gave Alex and the Jockey a quick glance, then looked back at the grubby thief on the ground.

"You been stealing things again," shouted their leader. "That's why we kicked you out in the first place . . ."

"I haven't been. I'm straight now."

"Just hit him," said the smaller of the attackers, raising his lump of wood.

Alex felt the Jockey tense beside him as the man started whimpering, holding his hands in front of his face. It was a pathetic sight, this praying for mercy. How could this sniveling old man be the "ghost" who had robbed him? Obviously the thief had used the dark to his advantage, tricking him with his voice, to give the impression he was menacing and strong. Alex felt a little stupid and ashamed. If there'd been more light around at the time he wouldn't have let this miserable old drunk take what didn't belong to him.

The three vigilantes paused, and the Jockey rocked back on his heels, a grin showing in the dim light. "Watch this," he said.

The old thief started talking fast, pleading in a high-pitched whine. "One of them dropped something, see?" he said, pointing to the boys. "And I was just doing the right thing . . ."

"Taking what isn't yours, you mean?" said the pack's leader. "You're a lying scumbag. We oughta beat some sense into ya."

"No, please," begged the grubby thief, falling backward onto his elbows as if he'd been hit. He turned to the boys again. "Come on lads, you'll stick up for me, won't you? Can't let these fellows hurt an old man . . ."

Alex was revolted by this performance, and he turned to the Jockey expecting him to feel the same, but he seemed expressionless. Then he saw that the Jockey's fists were balled and his muscles taut.

The three men laughed at the abject thief, kicking dirt into his face and cowering body. Then the leader shook his head and pulled on his smaller mate's shirt. "Come on," he said. "Fire's burning low."

His mate nodded, then nudged the third member of their party. "Coming?" he asked.

The third attacker nodded, then kicked the man savagely in the shins. A great howl erupted from the grubby thief as he clutched his legs, moaning that they were broken. The man who'd kicked him laughed, then headed off with his friends. All three walked past the spot where Alex and the Jockey stood, looking straight through them as if they did not exist. They vanished back into the trees, the moans and cries of their victim echoing behind them.

"Anyone would think they cut his throat," muttered the Jockey.

"Come on," said Alex, motioning to the departing men. "Let's go back to that fire. I'm freezing."

"You kidding?" said the Jockey. "This is the piece of snot who stole your jacket."

Alex looked at the grubby thief, still prone on the ground and sobbing loudly, his shoulders rising and falling with dramatic misery. He took a step toward him, then shrugged. The old guy got what he deserved. As for the jacket, it didn't seem to be anywhere in sight. Maybe they'd get lucky and find it in the woods.

"He's just a pathetic drunk," said Alex. "Let's leave him . . ."

"He stole from you."

"Who cares?"

"Who cares?!" shouted the Jockey. "What kind of wuss are you? *You* care. Never let anyone take advantage of you. Someone takes something from you, you take it back. They steal your money, you make them poor. They steal your life away, you make sure you steal theirs a hundred times over!"

Even in the darkness, Alex could see that crazy look in the Jockey's eyes again. There were no choices being offered here, no options about what to do next. The Jockey was making it very clear what he expected of his student, and Alex didn't feel inclined to refuse him. He looked at the old man rolling from side to side, clutching his shins. It reminded him of some of the international soccer stars he'd seen on the TV, playing for a foul. They always seemed to bounce up and run once the ref wasn't interested.

He took a few steps closer to the thief, guessing he was about his father's age. What the hell had happened to him to get like this?

"Hey!" shouted Alex.

"That's the way," said the Jockey.

"Hey, you! Where's my jacket?"

The man didn't answer.

"Kick him," urged the Jockey.

"No way."

"You want *me* to?"

"No," said Alex. He took the final few steps to the thief and prodded him with his foot, but all it produced was another loud burst of wailing and sobbing, as if he'd stuck him with a red-hot poker.

"The guy's had it," said Alex. "Let's just leave him . . ."

The Jockey looked down at the miserable wretch on the ground. "They tested me in Barlow," he said. "Stole some little thing from me, just to see how I'd jump. I let it slide the first time. Next time they did it, I reacted. Found the prick who done it and cut little holes in all his prison clothes. Shoulda heard the yelling he got the next day." He nodded to the man on the ground. "So, you got to react."

"What more do you want me to do?" asked Alex. "Every time I touch him he squeals."

The Jockey shrugged. This was the pupil's problem again, the teacher would just observe. Alex sighed, then looked for a spot to kick the old man. It wouldn't be too hard, just enough to satisfy his "teacher." He drew back his leg and was ready to strike when the old man lashed out viciously with his legs, scissoring Alex and sending him sprawling to the ground. He hit hard, landing on his backside. The "wretched," grubby thief was over him now, fists clenched, shaping up.

"Little punk!" he yelled. "Little snot-head . . ." Now *that* was the voice that Alex had heard in the darkness. The anger, the cunning, the malice, they were all back. "Kick me, would ya?" he yelled.

His fists looked like clubs, vicious, grubby rocks that could smash a face. Alex tried to get his arms up for protection, but they were neatly pinned by the thief. He rolled his head away, looking at the Jockey, who stood with a keen, almost excited expression on his face.

"Do something!" yelled Alex.

His teacher shrugged again. "You do something."

"Just frigging help me!"

"You don't need help, little Alex."

The thief shifted his position, crushing Alex's chest, grinding him into the ground.

"He's hurting me . . ."

"Crack a joke," said the Jockey, a half smile on his face. "Say something funny . . ."

A sudden rage exploded in Alex. "Shut up!" he screamed.

"What? Are ya angry with *me* now?" sneered the Jockey. "I ain't the one sitting on top of you . . ."

Alex looked up to see the old man was leering down at him. He seemed to be enjoying the Jockey's taunts, as if he was somehow in on a secret, sly joke. Something snapped for Alex. How dare they do that? How dare this disgusting old fart sit on him with that superior look on his face? How dare the Jockey just make smart comments? How dare anyone treat him like he wasn't even there?

He rolled and kicked, yelling with a rage that was like a fire inside him. It burned right through him, consuming all the dread and fear and weight of the past months.

"That's it," said the Jockey, moving closer, eyes alight with Alex's rage. "That's what ya need . . ."

Alex bucked some more, dislodging the old man slightly. Once the weight had shifted he had a lever to push him even further. "Move! Move!" he screamed, rolling the thief further. He seemed to have a strength he never knew existed. His arms were powerful, his body a brick wall.

"That's the Alex I wanna see!" yelled the Jockey.

He wound himself into muscle and intent and pushed the old man off, sending him crashing to the side. For a brief moment, Alex caught an expression in the thief's face, a look of satisfaction perhaps? He shut it out, shouting, "Hey! Not so smart now, are ya?"

The thief scrambled to his feet, and Alex followed, an incredible buzz surging through him.

"Not so frigging tough at all!" he shouted.

The Jockey was clapping his hands, saying, "Yeah," over and over. The old man gave him a quick glance, then turned and ran.

"Chicken!" yelled Alex. "Weak as . . . Wuss!"

How easy was that? He'd pushed the guy off, thrown him backward. He'd won! The Jockey came over and grabbed Alex in a strong hold, shouting in his face, "Little tough guy, eh? Little tough man!"

"He was weak!" shouted Alex. "Weak!"

And the Jockey laughed, but not at him this time. He laughed with a crazed joy, with the pride of a father for a son.

"Man, you done it," said the Jockey. "Man, you're there. You made it . . ."

They whooped and yelled until they were hoarse, until there was nothing left to yell about. Alex stopped. He stood still, the Jockey beside him. So close he could almost feel the rise and fall of his chest, so close he could smell the odor of his sweat, his meaty body. Then the Jockey stepped back.

"You remind me of someone I almost forgot about," he said, eyes bright with a glittering wetness. "Little bro. This has turned out better than I ever thought it would."

He placed his arm around Alex's shoulder—warm and strong. Alex felt a connection, not just to the Jockey, but to a thousand other heartbeats. They offered him promises, spoke to him about their power, their strength, their own courage when it mattered.

He knew then what had happened, knew it as sure as he was standing in that cemetery. This was no imaginary line on the road he had crossed now. This was a place that he'd only ever been able to watch from a distance. Now he could walk in. Now he could join with the band of brothers the Jockey spoke of.

Now he had a purpose.

"What about ya jacket now?" said the Jockey.

"We'll chase that old bastard down and get it," he said, voice calm.

"You bet," said the Jockey, gripping him tighter. "You frigging betcha."

CHAPTER THIRTEEN

They were headed for the city in search of the thief and the black jacket. This was the plan they'd come up with after a session of "school" with the Jockey asking Alex to think about where they'd find the old man, then laughing at every suggestion he made. Such was the style of his "teacher." It soon became obvious that the Jockey had figured out for himself which way they should go.

And so they walked again, retracing some of their earlier steps. It gave Alex a chance to go over in his mind what had happened in the cemetery. They were bland details compared to the feeling that buzzed through him as they walked. A power had been transferred to him. Alex could feel it, could taste it, even. His arms felt stronger, his back straighter, his head higher. He stepped now in time with that power, pacing with the prowling menace that walked beside him. It was as if a hundred voices sang for him, their deep vibrations rippling right through him. He could hear what had been silent. Could feel what hadn't touched him.

For the first time he could remember, he felt right, walking with his guide. Teacher and student. Older brother and younger brother. Father and son.

That was how it was.

If there had been a way for him to touch the Jockey now, to reach out to him and offer thanks, he would have done it. There wasn't.

The Jockey stopped walking, and Alex looked up to see that they had come to a big park that sat on the fringe of the city. By day it would be teeming with people, alive with families sitting on the grass, teenagers hanging around the fountain, or older people just strolling by. And at night? At night there'd be trash cans full of their refuse. Easy pickings.

"That's where he'll be," said Alex.

The Jockey slapped him on the back. "Then let's go."

He moved now with a purpose, patrolling the perimeter of the park, searching in the shadows and the lit areas for his prey. He felt connected to something deeper than this moment. He couldn't put words to it, he just knew in his bones that there'd been a thousand other such moments throughout time. It was such an incredible feeling, this connection, as if he was *all* there. He wondered if the Jockey felt it as well. Or had he felt it in Barlow?

"Tell me more about the brothers," he said, turning to the Jockey. "At Barlow."

The older boy didn't speak at first, just kept walking. Then, after a minute, he said, "Whatya wanna know?"

Alex grunted, annoyed that he had to explain his question. He just wanted to know . . . everything. What they said, what they did, what they spoke like. He was hungry for detail, imagining them with the Jockey, teaching, caring. And then it came to him. The real question. He knew he couldn't ask because the Jockey would just laugh at him, call him a girl. What he wanted to know was, did the brothers mean more to the Jockey than he did? Instead he went for the bland. "What were they like?" he asked. "You know . . . Having a bunch of guys around you like that . . . What's that like?"

The Jockey turned to him, a softer expression on his face. "You're all right, you know, little Alex. Them bastards at school, they just go for you because you're there, like. It's just the way you carry on. Could be anyone. That's how it works."

Alex nodded, not quite sure what the seniors at school had to do with the brothers at Barlow.

"There's always gotta be someone that's the dog, you know?" said the Jockey. "The one everyone wants to kick. Happens all the time."

He thrust his hands into his jacket pocket and quickened his pace. Alex felt a shiver and blamed it on the night air, which was getting colder. He stepped up his pace to catch up, thinking about the Jockey's words. *Was* he a "dog" for the seniors? A kicking bag? He wanted to say no, to resist, but now he saw how it was.

"No more for me," he said.

The Jockey turned to him. "What?" he said.

"No more . . . like . . . dunking and that. Not after tonight. I've . . . you know . . ." He wanted to explain the feeling he'd had back in the cemetery, the connection he'd felt, but he struggled for words again. How could he say the right thing without turning it into a joke? Then an image came to him and he grinned, adding. "I got a spear now."

The Jockey stopped and grinned back at him. "Yeah, maybe you have. Too bad it's only an eensy, weensy little spear . . ."

Alex protested at the joke, slapped the Jockey playfully on the arm. The Jockey went for a headlock, but this time Alex was quick. He darted away, laughing, running toward the fountain when he saw what they'd been searching for. It was the old man, loitering near an overflowing trash can, waiting for a crowd of Japanese tourists to vacate the area so he could get near the thing. The Jockey landed a new attack as Alex stood and watched his enemy.

"He's over there," said Alex, wriggling free from a headlock.

Now both boys watched the thief in action. He had a canvas bag slung over his shoulder, and Alex knew that his jacket would be in there somewhere. He wanted to run up to the old guy and snatch the bag from him, but the Jockey reminded him just how cunning the old thief was.

"You run at him like that," he said, "and you'll be eating dirt in the gutter. Na, we gotta plan this. Keep on his trail, don't let him slip. Keep him red-hot."

So they circled around the park again and sat on a bench seat. It seemed incredible to Alex that they found him so quickly. The Jockey had said they had to think and see and hear like their prey. Now they had him. Alex kept the old thief "hot" in his sight, but the waiting was driving him nuts. He wanted to act. The longer he sat the more his anger and energy faded. He blamed it on the cold night air, which was definitely closing in, freezing him slowly by each dropping degree. It was way below any comfortable temperature. Alex's T-shirt was a thin defense against its piercing fingers. The Jockey was okay, he still wore his jacket, buttoned up now against the chill. He looked quite re-laxed. Obviously his stomach wasn't growling with hunger and pain, either. Alex wished he'd eaten some of the fries when he had the chance.

Fine sprays of mist blew over them from the fountain, as if it was mocking Alex for dressing in such flimsy clothing. A large group of people sat on the grass to their right, drinking from bottles in paper bags and playing guitars. The soft singing wafted past them over the fountain's roar, soothing music, even if it was country western. Alex wanted to blot it out, to resist its gentle influence, but it stayed on the air at a nagging volume so that he couldn't ignore it. Each time a song finished there'd be laughing, or loud conversations, sometimes in a language that Alex couldn't understand.

He forced himself to think back to the cemetery, to maintain the rage he'd found there. He wanted to be like those guys around the campfire, tough, fierce protectors who lived in another world and didn't give a damn what outsiders thought of them. He admired the way they'd looked right through him as if he wasn't there. They were what the Jockey had been talking about. They'd crossed over the line into their own world—a place that would look like the world of the dead to ordinary people.

Alex wondered if he could actually go that far in his life, step into his own world completely. To be able to look right through people like his father, his mother, Marta; treat them as if they didn't exist. He grinned. There was no way Marta would put up with that. She'd pray to God, or bring around a truckload of chocolate biscuits!

He stood up, wiping the smile from his face. He needed to stay on the edge, stay hard and angry. It had been stupid to start thinking about Marta and home. How could he burn with the taste of chocolate on his mind? Now his head filled with their faces, like ghosts come to haunt him. They were smiling, warm, inviting him back home, away from his new world. He paced around, eager to get on with it, to take the old man down before his anger completely dissolved away.

"Whatcha doing?" asked the Jockey.

"Can we . . . like . . . just go after him now?" said Alex.

"I told ya . . ."

"Yeah, I know."

He sat heavily on the seat. What was the point of watching the old guy? They should just rush him and take his bag. No one would care. He was just an old drunk. A nothing.

The Jockey pulled his matches and packet of cigarettes from his pocket. He opened the lid of the smokes, then cursed quietly, crumpling the packet into a ball, which he tossed away. Then he flipped the lid to the book of matches, open and shut, its regular rhythm almost a soothing sound. "You know, I did see my old man one more time," he said.

He leaned forward, elbows on his knees, and Alex couldn't see the expression on his face.

"It was in this park," continued the Jockey, lighting matches and flicking them onto the path. "When I was only a little tyke, my mom used to take me here and let me run riot. I'd go chasing after people, you know, get food and stuff, annoy them, and they'd tell me how cute I was. Mom used to just sit on a seat, like, having a rest, I suppose. I was a wild little bastard by all accounts. Anyway, one day I was running like a half-cut goose and I stopped, saw this look on my mom's face. Real worried. So I asked her what was wrong, and she pointed to a group of dudes and said, 'That's your daddy over there.' I didn't stop to find out which one she meant. Just ran up to them and grabbed the nearest guy. Probably thought he looked right. She says I shouted at this guy, 'Daddy! You come home right now!' He just looked at me like I was crazy, and all the other guys burst out laughing. My mom grabbed me and took me home. Gave me a smack. Geez, I was a useless little kid, I tell ya. Yelled at the wrong guy."

"So, was your real dad in that group?" asked Alex.

"Yeah, I think so."

"And he . . . he laughed?"

"Yeah."

A cold wind blew across them, and Alex wrapped his arms around himself, thinking about the Jockey's father laughing at his own little son, never even knowing who he was. What a turd. What a low-life piece of scum. People like that didn't deserve to have kids. Didn't deserve to be loved. Not even God's love. He could hear Marta saying how God loves everyone. Alex wanted to argue with her, to shout, "What good is God if he just accepts anyone?" Marta made it all too simple. Some people were a mistake, a blot that needed to be wiped away.

A grub that needed to be taught a lesson.

He leaned forward, clutched his stomach, a sick wave of nausea washing over him. He could feel his eyes stinging and refused to allow them to make a fool of him, to give the Jockey something to laugh at. It was all right for Marta, she was happy. He wasn't. If he met this God, stood with him toe-to-toe, he'd ask Him why it had to be so hard. Why he had to feel this dead weight. Why he had to see in other people's faces the cold certain fact of what a useless screwup he really was.

It came to everyone's face eventually. Even Marta's. He remembered the way she'd looked at him when he'd said that he and the Jockey had a plan for the weekend.

Alex sat up. A thought suddenly chilled his mood. What if

Marta spoke with his father? Said something innocent that gave the game away? Even though she didn't know the details of the weekend, she knew enough to raise an alarm. He'd almost forgotten about her because she'd been away for half the week. And he'd been busy with the planning.

Marta was a potential problem.

Alex turned to the Jockey, debating whether to say something, until he realized that it would just earn him misery. No, he could handle this alone. There was a phone booth on the other side of the park. One quick call was all it would take. Set her straight, keep her quiet, then get on with the real work of the weekend.

He glanced at the old thief, still on the other side of the fountain, and he remembered the slap in the dark, the humiliation of shedding his jacket, the sly performance on the ground before he attacked. Some of the anger he'd felt before came back to him, and he smiled. That was more like it. Anger gave you so much energy.

Alex stood, shaking his leg. "Just gotta walk a bit, stay warm. Keep an eye on snot-brain, okay?"

The Jockey looked up at him, suspicious. "You chickening out?"

"No," snapped Alex. "I'm cold . . ."

The Jockey shrugged, putting his hands into his jacket pocket and turning away. Alex waited for a second, then walked down the path to his right. He couldn't go straight to the phone booth, that would really give the Jockey something to be suspicious about. He had to skirt around the park. It took forever, hugging the boundary, looking back all the time to check that the Jockey wasn't watching, stopping now and then to act nonchalant. By the time he arrived at the phone booth, he'd totally forgotten that he had no money for the call. He leaned his head against the plastic screen, laughing, because what else could he do? Tears came to his eyes, and he felt so exhausted that it was a struggle to stay upright. Everything was so damned hard.

The Jockey would tell him to toughen up in this situation, to meet the problem head-on. He straightened. With his stomach growling, and waves of nausea washing over him from hunger, he tried to think up a plan. He remembered that if you rang from a public phone without money, you got a second or two of connection before the phone cut off. Just enough time to say something, but what? He picked up the receiver and dialed Marta's number, listening forever to the ring before a sleepy voice, which he recognized as hers, answered.

"Hel . . ."

"It's Alex . . . !"

Click!

That was it. He wasn't even sure if he'd got his name out before the bar came down. What would Marta make of the call? That he was okay? That she didn't have to worry? Or would she panic, thinking he'd yelled his name in distress? Alex groaned. He hadn't thought that possibility through at all. He contemplated calling her again, but trying to shout something in one second would probably only make her panic more. Slamming the receiver in the cradle, he made his way back to the park bench. What a total disaster that had been.

He returned to the bench to see that everything had changed. The Jockey was no longer there, and the old thief had vanished as well. A white van was parked near the fountain, close to the group of country-and-western singers. Alex could smell coffee coming from the van, and he instinctively walked closer, seeing a small card table set up with plastic mugs and a plate of biscuits. There was a long Aboriginal word painted on the side of the van with some dot designs around it. He couldn't make out what it said.

A boy about the Jockey's age came up to the card table with a handful of empty mugs, which he dropped into a plastic bucket. He looked up at Alex and glared, hostile and suspicious. Alex said, "Hi," and the boy grunted, tidying up the table and brushing spilled sugar onto the ground. An older man joined the boy, pulling out a bag of rolls from the back of the van. Alex nearly moaned at the sight of them. The older man opened the bag, then looked up at Alex.

"You hungry, son?" he asked.

Alex nodded. "Yeah, I lost my wallet . . ." How easily he lied.

The boy rolled his eyes, clearly unimpressed by Alex's story.

"Here ya go," called the old man, tossing a roll in Alex's direction.

He caught it with one hand, then started devouring it.

"Bugger me." The man laughed, prodding the boy in the back. "He eats faster than you do, Max."

Max shrugged, then carried the bucket of empty cups into the van.

"Thirsty too, are ya?" asked the old man.

Alex nodded. "Yes," he said. Then he added, "Please."

"Polite, eh?" said the man, pouring him some tea from the urn. "Parents bring you up right?"

"I suppose so," said Alex, shrugging.

He accepted the mug of tea from the man, then put several sugars in, stirring it slowly. He wondered if this old guy was getting suspicious about a boy of his age out on the streets without any parents. Would he call the cops? Maybe he should drink the tea fast then get out of there.

One of the guitar players from the group approached the van

and asked, "Got any matches, Uncle?" The old man patted his pockets, then produced a cigarette lighter, which he handed over. The guitar player nodded, then went back to the group.

"He's real good on the guitar is Junior," said the man. "Knows every tune."

As if to confirm this praise, Junior started singing a slow, sad song, and a few other voices joined in with him. Alex sipped his tea, amazed that it tasted so good. He could feel his spirits lifting. Suddenly all the worry about Marta and the thief and his "job" that night washed away.

"My name's Alex," he said.

"Is that right, eh? You can call me Uncle, if you like."

Alex nodded. Max crawled out of the van and jumped to the ground. "So, how come you know Lonesome?" he asked.

"Who's Lonesome?" asked Alex, looking around. Was it one of the guitar players?

Max rolled his eyes, then muttered something to Uncle in another language. They both laughed quietly, then started packing up the tea things. Uncle tossed a biscuit at Alex, who managed to splash himself as he caught it. Luckily the tea had lost some of its heat.

"Shaved head," said Max. "Muscles. Tough guy . . ."

"Oh," said Alex. "You mean the Jockey."

Max burst out laughing. "Jockey? What's he riding? Some washed-up nag coming last at Flemington?"

"Na," said Alex, trying to sound tough the way the Jockey had taught him. "They call him that 'cause he's short. He probably could be a jockey, but I wouldn't disrespect him about it. Could give you trouble . . ."

"He's a jockey, eh?" said the old man, making himself some

coffee. "What's that make you, son? Jockey's apprentice? You ever ride? You're small enough for it, too."

Alex shook his head, and was about to say he didn't trust horses, when Max walked over and tried to take the unfinished mug of tea from his hand.

"Hey," said Alex.

"Looks empty," said Max, peering into the mug.

"Looks half full to me," said Alex.

Max smiled, sizing this little squirt up. "Tell me," he said. "Your jockey fella. He teach you how to fight?"

Alex took a deep breath. What had he got himself into now? He tried to think of what the Jockey would do in this situation. He'd bulk up, like he did when the brothers surrounded him at Barlow Road. Make an instant impression.

"He's taught me enough," said Alex, trying to puff out his puny frame. "I wouldn't mess with me, either. I've been inside Barlow Road, you know . . ."

Max's eyes widened but not with fear. An amazed look spread across his handsome face, then he burst out laughing. Uncle grinned at Alex, and asked, "How'd you get by in Barlow without breaking in two, son?"

Alex blushed deeply. Obviously they didn't believe him. He wondered if he should come clean but decided that it would only double his humiliation if he told the truth now. He tried to bluff his way out. "I can be tough when I have to. When I say something, I mean it. And when I do something, I mean it. And when . . ."

The old man held up his hand. "Okay, I reckon I get the picture. You better take a step back, Max. This is a desperate character you're dealing with here."

Max took an exaggerated step backward, warding off any potential attack from the "tough" Alex. Then he sat inside the back of the van and held his stomach, pained from laughing. "You must have been in a different Barlow from me, eh?" he said.

Alex groaned. Just his luck to try and lie to someone who'd actually been inside Barlow Road.

"Because I went to the one that Lonesome went to," continued Max. "And it *was* a tough kinda place. Ask your mate. He spent his time stuck in the corner, getting as far away as he could from all of us. He steered clear of the white fellas, and he steered clear of the black fellas. The only friend he had was the wallpaper, eh?"

Max stood, shaking his head, and walked over to Alex, patting him on the back in a patronizing way. "Just make sure you don't try and hit no one with them powerful arms of yours," he said. "You might do some damage." He walked off to join the group, sitting next to some younger singers who grabbed him playfully in a headlock.

Alex turned from Max to see that Uncle was still smiling at him. It wasn't mocking, but kind, almost welcoming.

"Why did he . . . ," began Alex. "I mean . . . What did he do to . . . ?"

"What did Max get into Barlow for?" said Uncle. "Stole a car. Stupid, like all them young ones, eh? Still, no way he shoulda been sent up for it. Burns my heart to see our boys in that place. You ever actually been inside, son?"

Alex shook his head.

"Inside's a strange story, I tell ya. Too many black faces. It's not right. Why do they have to lock our boys up all the time? Maybe they think that'll keep their streets nice and tidy, eh? Seems to me everything's about looking tidy. Yep, looking tidy and fitting in. You know all about that, son? You fit in where you come from?"

Alex wanted to nod, to say of course he fitted in, but Uncle's words sat uncomfortably with him. He sniffed, then nodded in the general direction of the park. "My mate," he said. "He calls me his little brother, and that. He hit a cop real bad with a bat, you know. That's why he went to Barlow . . ."

"That'd get him into Barlow all right," muttered the old man. "So, he's your brother, eh?"

"Yeah, but not my real brother. . . ."

"Oh, there's all sorts of brothers," said Uncle. "Brothers in arms. Brothers who got honor . . ." Uncle paused, staring hard at Alex, a worried look on his face. "Maybe you should run on home now, son, and forget about this fella, eh?"

Alex shrugged. "Maybe he's gone home himself," he said.

"Na," said Uncle, nodding his head toward the fountain.

Alex looked up to see the Jockey standing on the other side, staring at him.

"Been there for a while now," said Uncle. "He does look like you, eh? You could be twins. Watch that Lonesome, hear? Keep him in the light, because that's your best chance."

"Right, thanks," said Alex, handing over his mug.

"Don't mention it," said Uncle. "After all, we belong to the same tribe, eh?"

Alex must have looked startled, because the old man laughed. "I don't mean your skin, son," he said. He shook his head, still laughing, and carefully placed Alex's mug into the bucket. Then he walked over to the singing group without a backward glance. Alex waited for a moment, perhaps for an invitation to join them, or perhaps for a way out? Nothing came, so he walked toward the fountain, certain that the Jockey's eyes were boring into him, wondering what he'd been talking to the old man about.

A song broke out behind him. It was familiar. Voices joined in on the singing, some out of tune, some out of time. He knew the words, could have joined in himself, except his voice would have been out of place. It was *their* song, sung in a circle with backs turned to him. Closed against the strange little apprentice.

Alex sighed. Confusing thoughts clashed in his mind. Why did Max call the Jockey "Lonesome"? It didn't make sense. It had to be sour grapes, or something like that. The Jockey had probably given Max hell inside. In fact, Max was more than likely the one with the holes in his prison clothes. That would be it.

This thought lifted Alex's spirits, until he looked up at the Jockey. He *did* look lonesome, standing beside the fountain, fine sprays of water softening the air around him. Only his eyes were hard, and Alex knew that they spoke of an even harder heart. That was the true Jockey, no matter what some strange boy said. That was the Jockey who would guide him toward the job he had to complete that night.

Revenge.

CHAPTER FOURTEEN

They'd been walking for well over half an hour—the thief nowhere to be seen—heading toward a major freeway that ringed the city on two sides. Alex could see the glow of its amber lights, and the dull roar of the traffic was quite distinct now. A long bridge that formed part of the freeway stood out like a beacon ahead.

The walking had been hard, the tense silence between them deadening Alex's legs. Since the fountain, no words had been exchanged, just a quick command to "get going." All along the city streets and the wider, emptier roads, he'd looked at his teacher, "Lonesome" in a lonely place, knowing that Max's story had to be false. No way could he see the Jockey sitting alone in a prison yard or cafeteria. He was too strong for that. If they ignored him, then he'd rip them out of their tight little circle and make them see him.

But even with all the reassuring he gave himself, something still didn't add up. He couldn't put his finger on it, but there was a change in the Jockey, subtle but there. Maybe it was in his face or his jawline or the way he held his stubbly head. He stared at the Jockey, trying to pin him down.

"What are you looking at me like that for?" The Jockey glared at him, eyes hard.

"I'm not looking at anything," replied Alex.

"No?" said the Jockey, a mocking grin on his face. "Coulda fooled me. You've been staring at me ever since we left that park."

This was heading into dangerous territory, so Alex diverted him with an accusation of his own. "How come you didn't come over when I was at the van?" he asked.

"Wasn't hungry."

"Could have said hello."

"No point."

"There was someone there you knew," said Alex.

He glanced quickly at the Jockey, gauging his reaction, but there was nothing to see. His companion continued on, pointing to the large bridge, which loomed ahead of them. "There it is," he said.

They stopped.

The bridge spanned an industrial wasteland, carrying the freeway traffic over the empty warehouses and fenced-off wilderness. The city had been left behind, and now they stood among the ghosts of empty factories reflected in the nearby water, oily and dank. Traffic rumbled above, like discontented beasts, growling for all to clear a path. They were so small down here, just specks, dwarfed by the bridge's huge pylons. Alex looked at these concrete monoliths. One had small metal steps up its side, wrapped in a wire cage. This ladder led to a gantry that ran under the apron of the freeway, obviously an access area for any work that needed to be done under the bridge.

"Are we going over that bridge?" asked Alex.

The Jockey leered at him. "The bridge to nowhere, eh?" he said. "Or the frigging bridge to the pot of gold. What'll it be, little Alex?" He laughed, even though his joke was nowhere near funny, then nodded at the bridge and said, "There's someone up there wants to meet ya."

"Who?"

"Who do ya reckon?"

"You mean, you knew all along where to find him?" asked Alex.

"'Course I did," said the Jockey. "But I wasn't gonna tell you that. What good would it do leading you here by the hand? You had to work on your hunting skills . . ."

Alex felt the same confusion again. How had he worked on his hunting skills when the Jockey had led him to this place? Then he remembered the process of finding the thief in the park. That had been all his own work. Maybe the Jockey was simply saving time by taking him here. It seemed that everything was a test. Perhaps even his encounter with the thief in the cemetery. Maybe the Jockey knew that was where the old man hung out, looking for unsuspecting prey. Maybe the Jockey had thrown him into that danger, hoping it would all lead to this.

Alex looked up at the bridge. It wasn't the bridge to nowhere, it was his way into a world he'd wanted so badly back at the cemetery.

"You afraid of heights?" asked the Jockey.

"No," said Alex. In truth, the thought of climbing anything high did make him nervous, but he wasn't about to share that. It almost seemed as if it was some other boy who'd had his jacket stolen, not him. The cold drift of the night air was the only reminder that his adventure in the cemetery had been real.

The Jockey continued toward the pylon. He was in no hurry. Alex jogged to catch him, wondering if he should bring up Max and the "Lonesome" nickname again. He told himself to let it slide, that it didn't matter, but it did. He couldn't quite say why or how, but he had to know what Max had meant back in the park.

"Did you hear what I said before?" asked Alex when he reached the Jockey's side.

No response.

"Max," said Alex. "The guy at the park. He knew you in Barlow Road . . ."

"So?"

The Jockey sounded defensive, but then again, that was nothing unusual. Now what did he say? Accuse him of lying? Call him Lonesome? He struggled for words, allowing an uncomfortable silence to grow again. This time the Jockey broke it.

"You gonna say something?" he said. "Or are you gonna stare at me like a girl again?"

Alex took a deep breath but found no words. The irony of his situation didn't escape him. Alex the Lip, the Smart Alex, who could joke and quip and lay anyone flat with his tongue, was lost.

"I don't know," he said. "I just . . . you know . . . you said about the brothers, so I thought you'd wanna see him . . ."

The Jockey laughed at him, a callous expression on his face. "Oh, you frigging thought, did ya? Thought I'd run over and wet my pants because I seen another inmate from Barlow? Thought we'd hug each other and talk about the good old days? There were no good old days in Barlow!"

Alex had never seen such emotion in the Jockey's face before. He grabbed Alex by the arm, strong, and held his gaze. "Whatya think this is all about, huh? This whole night?"

"I dunno." Alex shrugged.

"You dunno!"

"Okay . . . it's about making me a man or something . . ."

"It's about you getting some frigging respect. Do you think I was joking when I said this would be hard? Huh? You're not gonna earn your respect sitting on your couch playing with a brick. You get it? You've been robbed. You've been laughed at. And now you gotta go as deep as you've ever gone before, little Alex. Now you're gonna get a taste of what it was like in Barlow Road. And when you come out the other side of all this, you think you're gonna want to go back?"

Alex shook his head, well aware of what the Jockey was talking about. If he followed this all the way, then he would have to make some hard decisions, and carry out some even harder work.

"Of course you ain't gonna want to go back. So now you see why I didn't rush over to Maxie boy."

His voice cracked for a mere second, broke the image of strength, and the Jockey released his grip, turning away from Alex, placing his hand momentarily to his face. There was a pause between them, a gap of time that Alex didn't dare enter. He waited for the Jockey to wipe away whatever it was he had on his face. When the Jockey turned back, he looked at Alex with eyes that just seemed old now. Then he walked off toward the bridge, his body tense, his gait even more menacing than usual. Alex stared at him, shivering, the cold eating into his bones. There seemed to be no protection from it now. He watched, miserable, until the Jockey stopped and turned, shouting, "Come on!" He was way ahead.

Alex moved, catching up to him at the bottom of the pylon. The Jockey was already on the first rung of the ladder. A wire enclosure began just above the Jockey's head. It completely surrounded the rest of the ladder, all the way to the gantry. There was a barrier a few feet or so up, a wooden roof that extended outside the cage and was fringed by loops of sharp, barbed wire. This barrier would stop anyone from accessing the rest of the ladder and making the full climb. It had a padlocked door, and the Jockey climbed up to it and gave it a rattle, as if he half expected it to be open. It wasn't. The Jockey climbed back down to the ground, looking back up at the enclosure. Just beyond the barrier was a hole in the wire that looked as though it had been cut or broken, obviously an access point created illegally. Someone climbing up the outside of the wire enclosure could easily get into that hole and access the ladder. But first they'd have to get over the barbed-wire loops that extended out from the wooden barrier.

Alex followed the Jockey's gaze, his neck straining as he took in all of the climb. He shivered, partly from the cold, partly from the dizzy spin his head was going into.

"Listen . . . ," he said.

"What's the matter? Chicken?" asked the Jockey.

"Na . . . it's just that . . ."

"He's up there, Alex," said the Jockey. "Your man. No witnesses. No chance for him to escape. . . . And best of all, you got surprise on your side. Can you taste what it might be like, to have that jerk saying 'sorry'? Can you imagine how you're gonna feel? You're gonna walk tall. Don't disappoint me, Alex. Prove to me that you got what it takes. Show me." The Jockey was almost whispering by now. "Then you'll know, Alex. You'll know what you got in here."

The Jockey jabbed him hard in the chest, creating an ache

over his heart that started to throb. Alex winced, but showed nothing, looking up again at the gantry for distraction. The Jockey was right. Up there was his man. But try as he might, he couldn't feel the same anger that he'd felt in the cemetery. Soon they'd overcome barbed wire to get at their prey. Soon they'd close in on the hunt.

"So, are ya ready?" asked the Jockey.

"Yes," said Alex with very little conviction.

The Jockey grinned, then started climbing the outside of the wire enclosure, heading for the barbed wire and the hole that lay beyond it. Alex followed, reaching out from the bottom rung of the ladder to grasp the wire and haul himself up. He clawed and gripped his way up the outside of the wire cage, his feet sometimes slipping. The Jockey had stopped above him, so he had to hang with his fingers through the wire, each strand cutting into his skin. Alex looked up to see the Jockey negotiate his way over the treacherous barbed-wire loops. With a push on his legs, the Jockey lifted himself as high as he could, then kicked a leg over the sharp wire. He balanced there, leg arched over the knife-edge, arms supporting the rest of his body. The strain made him quiver, and Alex could see beads of sweat dripping from his forehead. Next he inched his other foot up the wire, gaining height link by link until he was high enough to push himself forward and reposition his hands over the barbed wire and onto the wooden barrier. Here he paused, his stomach close to the barbed wire, and he kicked off, lunging himself over the edge and through the hole onto the safety of the barrier. The Jockey lay there panting, a big grin on his face.

The pain in Alex's hand grew too strong, and he dropped back down to the ground, feeling a sharp wrench in his ankle. He stood, testing it, and was relieved to feel it still holding him.

"Come on," called the Jockey.

Alex looked up. How the hell could he ever get over that barbed wire if he couldn't even hold on? "I can't do it," he said.

"I can't do it," mimicked the Jockey.

"Doesn't matter if you make fun of me!" shouted Alex. "I can't get over that barrier . . ."

"Of course you can . . ."

Alex started climbing the outside of the wire enclosure again, the pain burning in his hands. He reached the barrier where the Jockey was squatting, leaning out through the hole.

"Help me up," said Alex.

"No."

"What?"

"You gotta do it alone . . ."

"This is just crap!" yelled Alex, pushing himself higher.

It was too much, what the Jockey was asking him to do. He was taking him too fast and too far. How could he follow down this hard road, when he didn't even know . . . ? Alex paused, looking at his teacher, the sweat beading his brow. The Jockey. Lonesome. How could those two names sit together? He could see the barbed wire right in his face, close to his eyes. It was sharp, ready to cut him. It *would* cut him.

He dropped back down to the ground again, the Jockey's laughter mocking him from above.

"That guy back in the park?" yelled Alex. "Max. He said something. Said that you were a liar. He said you weren't even called the Jockey in Barlow Road . . ."

"Who cares what I was called in Barlow Road?" yelled the Jockey. "Get yourself up here."

"Were you called 'Lonesome' in Barlow?" shouted Alex. "Were you?"

The Jockey sighed, sitting back onto his bottom on the roof of the barrier, staring out over the warehouses. "Yes," he said in a voice Alex barely heard.

"So why didn't you say that in the first place?" called Alex.

The Jockey looked down at him, shaking his head. "You can be a little jerk when you want to be, you know that? Everyone is lonesome. It's a lonely, frigging life. Who have ya got? Eh? Just yourself. I mean, look at you. The only friends you got at school dip your head in the toilet. And now you're moaning to me about what Max said. Get over it. I never lied to you. I said the brothers taught me to be tough, and they did."

A sudden fury overtook Alex, and he climbed the wire enclosure, as if possessed.

"But what kind of brothers are they if they didn't even like you?" shouted Alex.

The Jockey shrugged. "Nobody likes anyone, little Alex. You spend most of your life drowning in crap. And then you see a way of getting your nose above the surface, so you take it. Them brothers in Barlow, doesn't matter if they're friends or enemies. I used them to stop from drowning. That's how it works."

Alex wanted to yell that the Jockey was wrong, that it wasn't as bleak as that, but what would be the point? He was stuck on the wire, about to go up and pay back an old drunk for stealing his jacket. He was at the gates of a dark and miserable place. He pushed himself up farther, poised with his chest at the sharp wire. His arms shook from the effort of holding himself up and the Jockey pointed to them.

"Lift yourself higher, it'll get you over."

"It'll cut my stomach," said Alex.

"Don't know that."

The pain in his arms was hot, searing him, shaking his muscles to jelly, but still he hesitated. "You made it sound like they taught you like you're teaching me," he said.

"Maybe they did," said the Jockey enigmatically.

Alex would not move, and the Jockey shouted, "Listen, you little dickhead! What do ya want from me? I'm trying to burn up the stupid frigging idiot who gets his head dunked because he's useless. I'm giving you a chance to prove yourself. Now, you coming or what?"

Alex looked down at the ground. It seemed much farther away now. Did he drop again? Or did he get over this barrier? With a scramble of his legs he lifted himself higher, but the wire started jabbing him through his T-shirt, ripping it in several places.

"This is nuts!" he yelled.

The Jockey smiled at him, but offered no assistance. Alex pushed farther with his legs, scraping his stomach along the wire. Sweat ran from his brow, dripping down into his eyes. It turned into freezing, bitter rivulets. His muscles quivered with strain, and his body shivered in harmony. Alex swore loudly. He *would* get over this barrier, just to stop this shaking, just to show the Jockey that he wasn't soft. He pushed more, and now he had one leg on the barbed wire, his jeans offering more protection. Balanced, he waited, not knowing if he had the energy to get the last of himself onto the roof of the cage. Suddenly he felt a grip on his belt as he was lifted up off the wire by the Jockey.

A hot, burning pain tore along his stomach, cutting through his T-shirt. Ripped by the razor, searing with heat from the wire's sting, he lay on the wooden barrier. Panting, blood running from his cuts, his arms and legs as weak as jelly. He lay looking up at the Jockey, who'd pulled him over the last of the hurdle. How strong was he, to lift him up like that?

"Hey, little bro," said the Jockey. "You are one tough little dude."

"Thanks," whispered Alex, still short of breath.

A warm agony trickled across his skin, and he sank into the comfort of it. The Jockey leaned down and smeared his hand in the grime on the wooden platform, then he wiped it across his own face. He repeated this gesture, darkening his face, masking himself in grim war paint until he was a silhouette fringed by the city-glow in the night sky.

Now he wiped some of the grime onto Alex's face. Darkened him, rubbed away his old features. Smooth, gentle strokes. Soft. Touch. Then he leaned forward and whispered, "Welcome to hell, little bro."

CHAPTER FIFTEEN

After a brief rest, they climbed the ladder to the gantry, which hung beneath the bridge. As short as they were, they still had to crouch to walk along the narrow framework. Alex wondered how a grown man would go trying to move along this tunnel under the bridge. They made slow progress, high above the ground with a 160-foot drop below. The only guard against falling was a small rail that looked flimsy indeed, and they placed each foot carefully for balance. Every now and then great gusts of wind would buffet them, threatening to blow them over the side. The concrete roof above offered no comfort, it shuddered and vibrated from the traffic, giving them a giddy feeling if they touched it with their heads. And when a truck went overhead, the deep *boom* of its wheels resonated right through them. The gantry couldn't have been used very often. It was littered with rat dung and other debris. Stuck away as it was, high above the ground, it was a perfect hiding spot for their prey.

"How do you know for sure he's here?" called Alex, fighting to be heard over the constant hum of the traffic.

"I watch and learn," answered the Jockey, now looking back over his shoulder.

They were more than halfway across the gantry, heading toward the next pylon. Alex could see a metal door cut into the pylon, and he wondered if that was just an access through to a gantry on the other side, or if there was a room cut into the concrete structure. Maybe a home for someone who liked to stay away from prying eyes? It would be an excellent hiding spot. The only sign that someone lived up here was the hole in the wire that they'd scrambled through to get to the metal ladder.

As they neared the opening into the next pylon, the Jockey slowed down, stopping about twenty feet from the door. He crouched on the gantry, and Alex joined him.

"This is it," said the Jockey. He spoke in a low voice, and Alex had to strain to hear him. "He hangs out inside there."

Alex looked past his mentor to see that the metal door was slightly ajar, beckoning to him. A black nothingness lay beyond it. "You ever been in there?" he asked.

The Jockey shook his head. Great. Nobody knew what they'd find when they entered. Would it be as dark as it looked? Was it the perfect spot for an ambush? This whole thing had a weird feeling about it. Why hadn't the old man seen their approach? Surely he'd have escaped by now, out another entrance perhaps?

"Go on," said the Jockey, thrusting his hands into his jacket pockets. "A fella would die of frigging boredom waiting for you to make a move."

"Okay," said Alex.

At the very least, he'd go in there and reclaim his jacket, stop this wind from cutting him in two. The Jockey swayed back as far as safety and comfort would allow, and Alex shuffled past him.

Once he was by, the Jockey said, "Look at ya. That little Alex, he's all but gone, eh? You burned him, man. Now you're a tough nut, gonna prove yourself tonight." Then he patted him on the back.

"You're not coming in after me?" Alex asked.

"Why? This is your man, not mine. You get him."

"I just thought . . ."

The Jockey sighed. "What are you gonna walk out of this weekend with? A scratch on your tummy? Or a real trophy? That guy there, he won't be easy. You know that. But you take him, and he's your prize."

Alex nodded, wondering if he should clarify with the Jockey what he'd meant by "take him." He decided against asking.

"Okay," he said.

"Yeah," said the Jockey, smiling. "Little tough guy, eh? You've got the smarts, don't forget that. You've learned plenty already. Even got yourself a frigging spear now. So use it, okay? 'Cause you'll need it."

Alex nodded, even though he hadn't been the slightest bit inspired by the Jockey's speech. In fact, all it had done was remind him just how cunning the thief was. So far he'd had two encounters with the guy. Round one he'd lost his jacket, round two his dignity.

And now for round three, thought Alex.

He rubbed his palms against his jeans, finding a small tear made by the barbed wire. Fiddling absently with the hole, Alex crept forward. His stomach ached, and the cold had returned to his body. He looked at the metal door. All he had to do was burst in or roll in or sneak in or . . . This was totally nuts. He'd seen enough movies to know that someone was always waiting on the other side of the door ready to brain you with a statue or a shoe or something they'd just picked up. Why was it that the characters in movies never knew this? They always waltzed into the darkened room without a care and *WHAM!*, they were knocked senseless.

Alex sighed. Fat lot of good knowing all that was going to do him. In this case, forewarned meant he'd be waiting for the blow. The only plan he could muster was to drop to the floor the minute he entered the place, and, hopefully, avoid being hit. With his mouth as dry as a desert creek, Alex walked cautiously to the doorway. A faint orange glow flickered from somewhere inside. He tried to peer deeper, but couldn't see anything significant. He took a breath, prayed that his head was harder than a statue, then burst through the door, dropping to his knees at the same time.

There was an almighty shout of, "Get the hell off me!" as Alex's legs hit something lumpy on the ground. No blow came, but the lump started to wriggle violently. It took him a second to realize that he'd landed on the thief, who had probably been asleep. This was perfect luck. The guy struggled, but he was wrapped up in a blanket and couldn't get his arms free. Alex pinned his shoulders, then leaned forward, positioning himself so that his knees dug into the man's throat. He looked down at his nemesis and grinned.

"Not so clever now, are ya," he said.

"Please don't hurt me . . ."

"I've seen that performance before, remember?" snapped Alex. "You won't fool me twice."

"Oh, I know," said the thief, a smarmy look on his face. "You're a smart kid, that's for sure. I could tell that right away. . . ."

"Bull!" Alex laughed. "It was pitch-black when we first met."

"I could tell by the sound of your voice . . ."

Alex could see more of the thief's lair, now that his eyes had adjusted to the light. The space was large enough for the thief to lie down with comfort. He was on a mattress of flattened cardboard boxes and had a fruit box as a bedside table. A couple of tea light candles sat on the floor, pinpricks of inadequate glow along the wall. But they were strong enough to illuminate the cartons of portable stereos, cameras, and other electrical goods that lined the wall to Alex's right. The thief had been a very busy old man.

Just beyond the bed was a dark, empty space. Alex stared at it, wondering what lay there, until he realized that it was a gaping hole. The pylon was hollow, and it didn't take a genius to work out that the hole dropped all the way to the ground. The thief noticed Alex's eyeline and smiled.

"Wouldn't want to slip down there, son," he said, a callous note in his voice. "You'd bounce a few times before you hit the bottom, then you'd splat open like a watermelon dropped from a tower."

"Shut up," said Alex. This was such a miserable bedroom. What if the old guy had a bad dream and rolled over? "Nice place you've got here," he said sarcastically. "You decorate it yourself?"

"Let me up, and I'll show you around," said the thief.

"No thanks. I can wait for the tour some other day. I'm after something that belongs to me . . ."

"No idea what you're talking about."

"Don't you remember? I lent you my jacket. You said, 'take it off' so you could borrow it, and I took it off. Now it's time to return it."

The thief laughed beneath Alex, showing his horrible teeth. "I remember a little boy nearly wetting his pants," he said. "That's what I remember. You couldn't get the thing off fast enough . . ."

"Shut up."

"Ooh, cut deep, did I? Miserable little brat, trying to be the tough man. Got ya dark makeup on then? Swaggering around like your mate out there. You're playing in the wrong league, boy. Think you've got what it takes, do ya?"

"Yep," said Alex confidently. "I do."

The thief smiled, the same leering grin from the cemetery, as if he was in on some secret joke. Alex felt his old anger return. How dare the guy act like he was in control? He leaned forward a little, putting extra weight on the old man.

"You're just a little twerp," said the thief, struggling a little to breathe. "Little snot, pissing and moaning about a jacket. Is this the worst you can do? Is this it? Come on, show me something that's gonna impress me."

"Hey!" shouted Alex. "I'm the one on top of you . . ."

"Not for long, son."

The thief started wriggling harder, bucking from side to side. Alex pushed down with all his strength and weight, aware that he couldn't hold him for much longer.

"How angry can you get, son?" sneered the old man. "Eh? How angry? Want a drink?"

He spat, lobbing an accurate, fast glob of spittle that landed on Alex's mouth and ran down his chin. "You disgusting old pig!" he yelled, slapping the old man in the face, blow after blow. Each connection made him somehow feel smaller, rather than in charge. Weaker, rather than stronger. So he lashed out harder until the ache in his arms and the throbbing in his fists convinced him that this *did* feel good. That this made him feel something. This *made* him.

The expression on the old man's face pulled him back abruptly from the madness. It was deadpan, detached from the blows and the pain, like a child's face that has suffered abuse again and again.

"You finished?" said the thief, his skin red from the blows. "Look what you've done to me."

Alex stared at the man's face. A deep, growing shame crept up on him, and he saw how futile and pathetic this all was. What did he gain from hurting this old, disgusting man? He could simply take his jacket now and be done with it.

"You're not worth it," said Alex, sitting back and wiping his mouth dry.

He reached over to the fruit box and found his jacket. Flicking it free, he tipped the box forward into the abyss. There were a few noises as it knocked against the side of the hole, then all was silent. Alex stared at the blackness, then rolled off the thief and crawled backward toward the door.

"Next time you pick on some kid," he said, "remember that you're old. You're disgusting and horrible."

The thief seemed unusually quiet and barely nodded.

"Is that all you got?" asked Alex. "Huh? Is that it? Look at ya. Wanna go home and cry to Mommy now?"

The old man turned his head away, as if he was crushed by these words. Alex grinned.

"You're beaten, man," he said.

And he'd done it. He'd defeated him.

"You took the wrong kid on, you ugly old pig."

The old man was still, mute, enduring the insults with his shoulders curled.

"In fact, you're so goddamned ugly," said Alex, slipping his jacket on, "that when you were born the doctor slapped your parents."

He was on a roll, too wrapped up in his own cleverness to notice that the thief was moving, carefully wriggling himself free from the blanket.

"So ugly, when you walk into a bank they turn off the cameras."

Too cocky to see the cold anger in the old man's eyes.

"In fact, you're so goddamned ugly, when you . . ."

The thief sprang at him, shouting, "Loudmouthed little punk. I'll kill you," pushing Alex backward onto the ground. Before the man had a chance to pin him down, Alex rolled to his right then scrambled to his feet. The thief ran at him again, heaving his shoulder into Alex's stomach. They crashed against the wall of cartons, and several fell forward, knocking them both on the head before clattering down the hole. Alex slapped at the man, but his blows glanced off his back, making no impact. The thief bent down and pulled on Alex's legs, crashing him to the ground next to the opening.

"Wanna go down there, eh?" shouted the thief. "Take your stupid jokes with you."

He pushed Alex toward the abyss, grunting with the effort.

"What are you doing?" screamed Alex. This was madness. He'd die. Murdered. A blind panic overtook him, and he swung his arms at the thief, smashing his fists against his head.

The man laughed at him. "Girly slaps!" he yelled. "Not so

clever now, are ya? Thought you'd come up here and show me something. You showed me what a disrespectful little jerk you are. A punk kid. A little nothing. A nobody . . ."

"Shut up!" screamed Alex.

"Maybe I should push you down the hole, eh? No one would miss ya. No one would cry. They'd probably be relieved that you're gone."

Alex bucked and kicked with a rage that was as furious as the anger that had exploded in him at the cemetery. Only this time it burned him up, ate away at his heart and soul. Its heat was the taunt of the old man, its fuel the picture of a nothing boy, a nobody, an insignificant waste. He wouldn't allow it to become real. Not after what he'd been through.

Alex threw the man backward then jumped onto him, lashing wildly with arms and legs and incoherent shouts. He could hear another noise in the background, a shouting voice, but it did not belong to the thief.

"Alex! Alex!"

It was just unnecessary static. The only thing that mattered now was the white-hot frenzy that consumed him.

"Alex! Cut it, okay? You done it. You got him. Come on . . ."

He struck with an incoherent fury, tears running down his cheeks.

"Alex! Get off!"

Blow after blow, until his arms ached and his hands were bruised.

"Frigging stop!"

The Jockey was yelling at him from the doorway, unable to get in, blocked by the old man's body. His hard-man big brother who had taught him oh so well. Was he urging him on? Telling him to hit harder? It wouldn't matter what he was saying, no human voice could reach Alex where he was.

"Hey! Alex! Stop it!"

The thief, who was huddled against the rain of blows, pushed away and made a dash for the exit, only to crash into the Jockey.

"Get out of the way!" yelled the man. "Little brat's gone insane . . ."

"I can't . . ." began the Jockey.

The thief didn't wait for any further explanation. He turned on Alex, a wildness in his eyes that would have been frightening at any other time. Alex had leaped to his feet now. They shaped up to each other, no exit from this madness.

The thief bellowed a wordless roar and flung himself at Alex.

Alex took a sharp breath.

There was no way he could match the power of the man's momentum.

He imagined the blow of the man's body against his. Felt himself being tipped, thrown, perhaps picked up and dropped down the hole. Given over like a worthless piece of debris to the harsh, cruel certainty of gravity.

As if it were a prediction.

He could see every tiny detail of it.

And so he acted instinctively. In a brief second before his next breath. As fast as a wild animal.

Alex took a step backward, rolling onto his back, his knees curled up. It was such a surprising move that the thief had no option but to follow, his momentum carrying him over Alex's head toward the abyss. There was a short, sickening scream, followed by a scattering of arms, legs, and feet, then all was silent.

CHAPTER SIXTEEN

Alex scrambled to the hole, peering into the blackness for any sign of the old man, but it was impenetrable.

"What the hell did you do?" yelled the Jockey.

"He was gonna kill me . . ."

"You frigging threw him down the hole . . . ?"

"I had to!"

"Jeezus!"

The Jockey was breathing in short, panicky breaths, his face red, his eyes wide with terror. Both boys leaned over the hole, searching through the blackness. They listened intently, and Alex thought he might have heard a tiny scraping, but no more sound came. He called out, "Are you all right?" his voice echoing around the abyss. As soon as he heard himself he realized how ridiculous he sounded. The man was gone, fallen 160 feet to a certain death. Tears trickled down Alex's face, and he sat away from the hole cradling himself, muttering that it wasn't his fault, that he hadn't meant for it to happen. A harsh voice spoke in his ear.

"What a frigging mess."

Alex ignored the sound. It didn't matter, nothing around him mattered. He'd killed a man.

"You've gotta get outa here now, Alex!"

Rough hands shook him, and he looked up through his watery vision to see the Jockey staring hard at him.

"Go on! Go! I'll sort this mess out," yelled the Jockey, but his voice sounded far off, from another place.

"I killed him," said Alex.

How could that have happened? How could he have caused someone to die? Perhaps the thief was still okay? Holding on to the edge, maybe? Alex crawled to the hole and started backing into its void, legs over the edge. The Jockey grabbed him by the T-shirt to pull him back, but it rode over Alex's head and threatened to come off.

"Stop it, you little moron!" shouted the Jockey.

He slapped Alex in the face, then grabbed him under his arms and hoisted him out of the hole. The Jockey looked back down into the darkness, then turned to Alex. "Run!" he shouted, pushing him toward the doorway.

"What about you?"

"I'll catch up with ya."

"But . . ."

"Run!"

Suddenly Alex's feet came alive. Run. Yes, that was what he had to do. Run like hell. This was murder. Get out of this evil place. He made his way across the gantry in half the time it had taken him to cross it earlier. The wind still blew, the way was still treacherous, but what did he care? He had to get out fast. When he came to the metal ladder he practically slid down the 160 feet, then rolled over the barbed wire without any caution. It might have cut him or torn his clothes further, he had no way of knowing. All his senses were numb, all his faculties concentrated on one thing only: running.

The vast wasteland flashed past him—empty factories, murky water. He ignored it completely. All he could do was focus on the way ahead, the way out. Soon the roads turned to streets, until he was back in the outskirts of the city. Then he stopped, his chest searing with pain, his lungs struggling to keep up. Bent over, fighting off waves of nausea that threatened to knock him off his feet, Alex leaned against a wall and sobbed. For how long, he didn't know. Several minutes, perhaps? An hour? Eventually he heard a familiar voice speak beside him.

"Jeezus," said the Jockey. He seemed a bit calmer now, breathing heavily from running, his face a mixture of excitement and awe. He sized Alex up, shaking his head. "You, like, threw the guy down the hole . . ."

"Shut up!" yelled Alex. "You wanna tell me something I don't know?"

There was a smugness about the Jockey.

"Little Alex," he said. "Man. Who'd have thought, eh? That you could be a killer . . . A murderer . . . They'll send you down, to Barlow Road . . ."

"Shut up! Shut up! A lot of help you were . . . Why didn't you let him pass?"

"Where the hell was I gonna go? Jump over the edge to let him by?" said the Jockey. "I mean, it was all over. Why'd you have to go psycho nuts on him?" Then he smiled. "Don't matter, 'cause it sure is frigging over now, eh?"

Alex closed his eyes, the horrible clattering sound coming back to him. "How can you smile about . . . about . . . that?"

"Wasn't me who killed the guy."

"What?"

Alex stared at the older boy, his so-called brother. Had he really just said that? Was he going to dump him now? "You're supposed to help me," he said.

"And I have," said the Jockey. "Jeezus, I didn't plan on this . . ."

"Of course you didn't!" shouted Alex. "Neither did I!"

"Okay, okay," said the Jockey. "Just stay calm." He stood and looked up the street, deep in thought, debating something in his head. Then he turned to Alex and said, "Follow me. I know what to do."

Alex looked at him. So far he'd dug him deeper and deeper into this mess. Could he trust the Jockey to get him out of it? What other choice did he have? He couldn't go home to his father. He had no one else who'd even have half a clue what to do in a situation like this.

Nodding meekly, Alex moved away from the wall. He thrust his hands deep into the pockets of his jacket, feeling something hard inside. A coin. Where had that come from? Was it his? Or did the old man put it there? Alex shivered, putting the coin back into the pocket. He didn't want to touch anything that had belonged to the thief. Rubbing his face, he said, "Let's go."

They headed back toward the city, and Alex kept an ear out for sirens, even though he knew there was little chance of the police finding the old man for days. That didn't stop him from leaping with fright when a taxi turned the corner, its amber light close enough to a police car light to give Alex a heart attack.

The Jockey seemed to know where he was going, and Alex followed without any questions. He was too exhausted to think.

All he wanted to do was curl up and sleep, forget this horrible night forever. He focused on the Jockey's back as they turned corner after corner, encountering passersby and street sweepers and packs of teenagers hanging around making loud noises that jangled Alex's nerves.

Eventually they turned a last corner, and the Jockey stopped. Alex halted behind him, his vision blurred with fatigue.

"This is it," said the Jockey.

Alex looked up to see a blue police station sign glowing above his head. He turned to the Jockey, about to ask what he was doing, and was met with the Jockey's hard stare.

"Enjoy Barlow Road," whispered the Jockey.

There was no time to think, no time to ask questions. Alex ran. A second later the Jockey would have had him in an unbreakable hold. He ran from the police station with the sound of laughter behind him.

"Little Grub!" called the Jockey. "They'll get ya in the end!"

Alex flung himself across a busy road, causing drivers to slam the brakes on their cars and lean on their horns. "Stupid kid!" yelled one man. Yes, he *was* stupid. But not anymore. Now he was a hunter being hunted, now he had to use every ounce of cunning he had to avoid the spear.

The city streets were no longer his. They were a hostile environment, a forest of hidden dangers and enemies. He had to get out, make his way to a safe haven, if only he could think of somewhere safe. The park? No, he'd been there with the Jockey. The cemetery? No way. The mall? Too lit up. He racked his brain for a plan or an idea, but the only image that came to him was of a happy face, warm, friendly, offering him biscuits, laughing along with him.

Marta.

How did he get to her? Then he remembered the coin in his pocket. She'd understand. She'd know that he hadn't meant to hurt the old man, that he was a good person, not a murderer. He ran to a phone booth, picked up the receiver and dialed her number, praying she would answer again. When at last he heard her voice he broke down and cried.

"Just come," he said to her. He couldn't tell her why. Couldn't bring himself to relive the death of the old man. She arranged a meeting place and had to repeat it several times. Finally it sunk in, and Alex let the phone fall free, running once again. By the time he reached the agreed place, his heart had frozen solid around the ripping shame of what he'd done.

He'd stopped crying, stopped feeling altogether. He was not going down for this. He was not going to Barlow. He wouldn't allow anyone to get close enough to try. He had to be hard now. Had to think of nothing else but his survival. Marta would bring him money, she'd buy him food. Then he'd move to the next step, and the next, until the nightmare was so far behind him he needn't think about it ever again.

CHAPTER SEVENTEEN

Against all odds, he slept. Curled in a darkened doorway, waiting the half hour that Marta said she'd be.

And he dreamed.

He was falling down a dark hole, his scream swallowed by the emptiness.

Claws scuttled against the walls, reaching out of the blackness to tear at his flesh. Rip his face. Scratch him open. An unbearable cold seared through him, icy fingers gripping his warm, soft inner body, tearing it out into the cold.

He was dying.

Death.

Then he remembered who he really was.

And he roared. Opened his mouth and lungs and roared so loudly that the whole world vibrated with the sound of it.

Scuttling talons receded into the night.

He woke.

Alex sat up, looking blearily at his gloomy surroundings. His head was still fuzzy from the dream, and his heart raced. Was it fear still? Or was it excitement that caused his heart to bang against his rib cage?

In his mouth he could taste something familiar. Salty. Primal.

It was the taste of blood.

THE HUNT

YOU GAIN STRENGTH, COURAGE AND CONFIDENCE
BY EVERY EXPERIENCE IN WHICH YOU REALLY STOP TO
LOOK FEAR IN THE FACE. YOU MUST DO THE THING
YOU THINK YOU CANNOT DO.

—ELEANOR ROOSEVELT

CHAPTER EIGHTEEN

The old wooden grandstand offered them shelter, but it could not keep the cold out. It was an open structure, with tiered hard benches long enough for them to lie on. The roof was tin, and seemed another world away, framed against the starry, clear sky. Marta sat in seat B5, staring out across the dark, murky playing field that stretched away from her. Alex lay along the seat beside her, his knees curled up like a little baby's, his fists clenched into tight balls.

They'd barely spoken to each other since Marta had pulled up in a taxi outside the hospital, where they'd arranged to meet. She had rushed out, half panicked, expecting to find Alex in a state of danger, or still crying and distraught. Instead he'd walked up to her with a hard expression on his face and said, "Got any money? I'm starving."

He'd seen the look of disappointment on her face, knowing

exactly what she'd be thinking—that he was just like the Jockey. He didn't care. He held his hand out, watching her reach into her pocket and pull out some coins. Then he'd run into the hospital and dropped the money into the vending machine, jabbing the buttons impatiently.

Marta had watched as he devoured two packets of potato chips in front of her without offering her any.

"So what's going on?" she'd said, once the last chip was gone.

"I don't want to talk about it," he'd mumbled.

"You're kidding. You call me in the middle of the night . . . I had to steal money from my dad . . . You were crying, Alex."

"Shut up!" he'd yelled.

Marta recoiled from the look in his eyes.

He softened slightly. "I just needed . . . I don't know."

"I can't help you if you won't tell me what's up . . ."

"Jeez, I wish I'd never called you!"

So she gave up asking, and they'd walked from the hospital toward the playing field, Alex with his hands thrust deep into his jacket pockets, staring at the ground. Whenever she'd tried to start up another conversation, he'd crack a joke, but they were cruel and unfunny.

When they'd arrived at the playing field, Alex had run to the stand and bounded up the wooden stairs to the back wall. Then he'd kicked and kicked at the wall, as if he was trying to put a hole in it. Marta had stood back, frightened, but eventually she told him to stop or he'd wake someone up in the nearby apartments.

Alex had glared at her, then stomped down to the front of the stand to sit with his knees up and his head buried between them. Once again Marta had tried to ask him what had happened, but he mumbled, "I don't want to talk about it." That had been almost half an hour ago, and in the time between, Alex had laid down on the bench and fallen silent, staring at the wooden barrier before him.

Marta sat wide awake by his side, her mind running through so many horrible possibilities. Now what was she going to do? Sooner or later her parents would notice that she was gone and panic. She hoped they found the note she'd left. Alex started mumbling beside her, arguing with someone in his head. Suddenly he sat up and said, "I know he's dead!"

"Who?" said Marta, her voice thin, as if the life had been sucked from her. She was stiff, frozen by the words Alex had uttered. They rebounded back and forth, until she added, "The Jockey?"

He ignored her question, stretching his legs, flexing his muscles, looking down to see if there was any sudden improvement. His arms were pale in the moon-glow, but maybe there was a hardness in his biceps now. Good. He had to tough it out. Hadn't the Jockey taught him that at least? He had to use his survival skills and walk the fine line through this mess to come out clean on the other side. No way would he go down to Barlow. It wasn't even his fault!

If he kept his head, no one need know about what happened to the thief. Alex didn't reckon the Jockey would say much, despite his prank with the police station. Not when he was on probation, and would wind up back at Barlow just for being out alone at night. The more he thought about that stunt, the more he hoped it had been the Jockey's way of welcoming him into the Barlow crew. He could have been actually accepting him in his own twisted way!

The only other proof of his crime that night was the body of the old man. Alex shuddered, remembering the sound of the clattering, the awful silence that followed. He shut his eyes. He had to be strong. Had to keep out useless stuff like feeling scared or feeling sad. But he couldn't. A lurching nausea washed over him.

"Goddamn it!" he shouted, just to shake off the feeling.

"God won't damn anything for you," said Marta quietly.

"Oh, very funny."

"You're really different," said Marta.

"Yeah? Well, you would be, too."

"Would I?" she said. "Who knows? You won't tell me what happened, so maybe I would be different. In fact, maybe I *am* different!"

"What's that supposed to mean?"

She didn't answer, just stared up at the sky, as still as granite.

"Whatya looking at?" he asked. "Is that heaven up there?"

He followed her gaze, amazed at how many stars there were. There were supposed to be shapes in the stars, patterns, but they looked like dots to him, nothing more.

"Do you ever see those things in the stars you're supposed to see?" he asked. "You know, belts and archers and stuff like that?"

Marta shrugged. "I don't want to talk about the stars," she said quietly.

"I mean, look at them," said Alex, ignoring her. "There's no frigging belt or bull or whatever up there. They're just stars, that's all. It always pisses me off the way they say you can see those shapes. They just made it up to show off or something, or to make dumb kids like me feel even dumber."

"You're not dumb," said Marta.

"No?" said Alex. He snorted, then added, "There's stuff you don't know."

She turned on him, furious, and hit his arm. "Stop it!" she yelled. "Either tell me what happened or say nothing. It's horrible. Someone's dead, but you won't say who. It's like *you're* showing off when you do that."

"I'm not showing off."

"Oh no? 'There's stuff you don't know.' You know who you sound like, don't you?"

Alex turned away from her, rubbing his arm. "You hurt me . . ."

"Do you?" shouted Marta, growing redder in the face.

"You're stupid," yelled Alex. "You know that?"

He stomped out of the stand and onto the playing field, kicking the grass with fury and stubbing his toe in the process.

"Ow!" he yelled. "Now look what you made me do!"

"Good!" shouted Marta. "Maybe you could stub your other toe, too."

Alex tried to think of something else to yell at her, but nothing witty or cutting came to him. She didn't understand about the Jockey. No one did. The Jockey had taught him stuff tonight, things nobody had ever bothered to show him before. Sure, it was dangerous, it was always dangerous with the Jockey's way of life, but there was no way he was going back to the old Alex. What had the thief said to him: He was out of his league? He'd show them all how wrong they were.

"I actually felt like I was somebody tonight," he shouted. "And you can't make me not feel that, okay? Why does everything have to be so screwed up? The one time I feel big . . . feel like I know how to handle it, and it all turns to crap."

It wasn't his fault that the old man had fallen into that hole. He shouldn't have come at him. Alex convinced himself that he had been right to fight back, protect himself. He pushed away the awful truth that he'd kept it going with his stupid taunts when it had all been over. That wasn't his fault, was it? He did what he had to do. He *was* a man. He was tough.

Then he remembered the grin on the Jockey's face, standing under the police sign. He saw the cruelty of the moment and pushed that away as well. There was an explanation for it. It all made sense. It *had* to make sense, otherwise the whole night had been a load of nothing. The Jockey's prank at the police station was part of the game. You play with a lion, you're gonna get a swipe now and then. They play for keeps. That was all it had been. A dangerous, cruel, but playful swipe . . .

Marta was standing beside him now. Alex tensed. Would she yell again? She seemed to have calmed down. Alex turned to her and said, "Look at me." He waited for her to meet his eyes. "I happen to like how I've changed, okay?"

Marta showed no emotion, just searched for him behind the hardness of his expression. Eventually she said, "Is this what being 'big' is like?"

"I don't know," he said. "It's what standing up for yourself is like. It's what being a man is . . ."

"Then you probably don't need me anymore."

"Probably," said Alex.

She closed her eyes for a brief moment, then turned and walked from the sports ground. Alex watched her, a small figure under the millions of dots in the sky. Why didn't they pierce her the way they pierced him? Why didn't they cut her through with light? He felt so lonely under this sky. An insignificant little patch of darkness, receding, vanishing into the shadows.

"Marta," he called.

She stopped. "What?"

"I dunno . . . just . . . you know . . ."

Marta turned and walked back to him.

"The Jockey said he'd be my big brother," said Alex when Marta reached him. He was staring down at the ground and could see his shadow on the grass from the moon. Incredible. A rock hurtles around in space and reflects the sun's light onto a boy's back, a whole lifetime away . . .

Marta didn't say a word.

"He said he'd teach me to spit fear in the eye . . ."

He could see Marta's shadow as well, her body blending into the shape of his. They were a dark shadow of two kids.

"I wrote a note to my parents when I left," said Marta. "But I couldn't figure out what to put in it, so I just said that I loved them, and I had to do something. That if I didn't do it, I'd probably hate myself. It's weird, but I guess I've changed, too. I stole from my father. I took his mobile phone, his money when he was in the shower. I broke a commandment, but I *had* to."

Alex turned to her, a tough, defiant look on his face. "Your dad will get over it . . ."

"I did it for you."

He looked back at the shadow, shaking his head. "What if I tell you what happened," he said. "And you hate me or something?"

"I can't hate you," said Marta.

"Why not?"

"Because I'm too cold."

He laughed, despite himself, and she joined in.

"Okay," he said. "Let's go back and sit down. It's even colder out here, for some reason."

They walked back to the grandstand, her arm rested against his, as if she was afraid he might suddenly float away. They were two friends again, sitting in the front row, just Alex and Marta, with a myriad of lights overhead, individual brilliance forming no particular shape at all.

CHAPTER NINETEEN

It was Marta who suggested they return to the bridge. Alex had told her about the struggle with the old thief and the fall down that horrible blackness. He changed the story slightly, left out the fury of his madness, depicted it as a fight over the jacket. That was close enough to the truth. As close as he could comfortably go, at least.

Marta sat listening, as still as stone. Then he came to the part where he'd wanted to climb down the hole to see if the old man was alive or not, and how the Jockey had pulled him out, then yelled at him to run.

Marta leaned forward and said, "Oh, Alex. What if he's still alive . . . ?"

"How can he be?" said Alex. "You didn't see how far he fell." He picked up an empty aluminum can, crushing it in his hand, seeing only too well how far that man had fallen. Seeing it again and again . . .

"But," said Marta. "You were right to do what you did, to at least try and see if he was okay."

"Was I?" said Alex, cracking the can, twisting the flimsy metal out and in. It made a harsh, awful sound, and he could see that it grated on Marta's nerves. "Everything I touch turns to crap," he muttered. "Dead, useless crap." He threw the can onto the playing field, disappointed that it made no noise as it landed. "I can't go back. Not to that bridge, not ever again. To go into that place . . . I . . . Marta, I did the worst thing. The worst thing ever . . ."

"He might be all right," said Marta. "You don't know. If you do nothing, then you're just running away."

He wanted to grab hold of her, his old friend, plead with her to make it right, to lift the weight that threatened to crush him. Every part of his body felt heavy, dragged down by a sapping force that refused to let him go. If he could, he'd curl up, close his eyes, and pretend nothing had happened—no night, no stars, no old man's body lying at the foot of the pylon—but he couldn't close his eyes, afraid of what his dreams would reveal to him. More than just the horror and the ghostly images of the dead; there was the roar of that creature, the taste of blood. They shamed him, whispered truths that he refused to listen to.

Alex balled his fists into his eye sockets, shuddering now and then, waiting for the flood to subside. "Promise me you'll never tell anyone about this," he said, voice muffled in his hands. He waited for her to say it, but only heard her sigh. "Promise!" he yelled.

"Oh, Alex, how . . . ?"

"No one, Marta," he said, lifting his hands from his face and looking at her. "No one, not even God."

Marta wiped her eyes, pushing away a tear. "I promise to be your friend," she said, smiling at him bravely. "Everything will work out. Come with me to the bridge. It's the right thing to do . . ."

"So what?"

"So . . . So, sometimes you have to do the right thing, even when it feels bad." She took hold of his hand.

"And you're absolutely sure of that? There's no, like, out-clause or something? No rules that say you gotta do the right thing, except for when it's really serious, scary stuff?"

"It's the really scary stuff that you *especially* have to do the right thing about . . ."

"How did I know you were gonna say something like that?" said Alex. He stood up from the wooden bench, his butt numb, his legs frozen, and shook himself awake. "I'm sorry, Marta," he said. "I can't." He started walking down the steps of the stand.

He felt alone again, leaving the stand behind, walking across the dewy grass of the playing field, soft and forgiving under his feet. He skirted around the front of the building, heading for a small gate in the fence that was down the side of the stand. It was aimless walking at the moment, but he was vaguely aware that he was headed in the opposite direction to the bridge.

After a moment, Marta joined him. She grabbed his arm and wheeled him around.

"Where's the bridge?" she asked.

"Huh?"

"The bridge. I'm going, even if you're not . . ."

"What would you wanna do that for?" asked Alex, shaking his head.

"I don't expect you to understand," said Marta.

"You're right," he shouted. "I don't."

He shuffled from foot to foot, the cold seeping through his shoes into his feet. It was time to move, get out of here. Not have this dumb conversation. Marta didn't understand the way life worked. You never got far doing the right thing. That was so obvious. Especially when everyone else around you did their best to walk all over you. The Jockey had shown him that. Look after yourself. After number one. After Lonesome.

Marta was smiling at him, an almost superior expression on her face. It unnerved him. Normally she was trying to make him feel better or was trying to cheer him up. Now she seemed so . . . independent. Was it for real? Surely she didn't really mean to go to the bridge alone? But there it was, that look of determination in her face.

Obviously she did.

"It's just stupid for you to go," he said.

"Oh, and it's not stupid for you to run away?" she snapped. "Come on, I don't have time. Where's the bridge?"

"Down by the docks. But you can't go on your own. It's like, dangerous."

She turned and started walking away toward the docks area.

"Marta? Marta?"

There was no response. No turning back. She just continued walking, ignoring him. Then he shouted, "Yeah, that'd be right. You're so desperate to be the good girl."

Marta turned and marched back to him. She grabbed him by the jacket, wrenching him in much the same way the Jockey had done, only she was not as strong.

"What are you doing?" he said, squirming.

"Is that what you think?" said Marta, a menace in her voice.

"Let go of me . . ."

"Is that what this is all about?"

He'd never seen such an expression on her face before. Maybe it was the lack of sleep or the stress of the evening. So much anger, mixed with a grim determination.

"Being good?" said Marta, almost whispering now. "'Cause I thought this is all about being tough. Isn't it?"

He couldn't concentrate on the question. Seeing his normally placid friend act in this way was too unsettling. "Marta," he said. "This is a bit embarrassing . . ."

"About being brave, Alex?"

"Marta . . . please . . ."

He could have pushed her away, smashed her hands free, but it wasn't her strength that held him there. It was the realization that even if he did break free, she'd still win. That the force of her argument, of her will, was stronger than any muscles.

"Marta," he said, "I dunno anymore. Just stop this, okay?"

She held his gaze for a second longer, then released him, walking over to the grandstand. Even in the darkness Alex could tell she was shivering, but he no longer cared. A hot anger started burning in him. How dare she humiliate him like that? He straightened his clothing, furious with her. "Jeezus!" he snapped, kicking the dirt.

"Leave him out of it!" shouted Marta back at him.

"I don't get it," he yelled. "All this stupid be brave, do the right thing crap!"

"Well, I'm sorry for you," said Marta, a genuine note in her voice.

He might have tried to carry on with the argument, or perhaps leave her there, but a bright light shone in his eyes. Marta squealed with shock, but Alex squinted past the glare of the flashlight to see an elderly woman in a thick bathrobe and fluffy slippers, a determined expression on her face.

"The residents around here are sick to death of your vandalism . . ." she said.

"We're not vandals," snapped Alex, tough, aggressive, the way he'd learned. "So get out of our way." He hoped there was also some menace in his voice.

"I've called the police," said the woman.

"Oh, hell," muttered Alex.

"Alex?" said Marta.

"It's okay," he said. The only other way out was back across the oval, toward the docks area. Could he walk in that direction? Take those steps?

"Come on," whispered Marta, glancing quickly at the old woman.

She shone her light on Marta now. "You don't look much like a vandal," she said. "This is a heritage grandstand, you know. History. My ancestors built this."

"Alex?" said Marta, a more urgent note in her voice.

"All right," he said. "Let's go . . ."

"You're coming with me?"

He glanced back at the woman. There were several other people on the street behind her, each wearing a bathrobe and slippers. It was a pajama vigilante group, armed with flashlights.

"Okay," he said. "I'll come with you. Or you can come with me. Whatever. We'll do it . . ."

"Alex, that's great," began Marta.

He didn't wait for her to finish. They had to get out of there fast. Taking her hand, he started running across the oval.

"I know which way you're headed," shouted the woman.

"The police will catch you. We're sick of your types, you hear? This is history you're destroying. History!"

As his heart pounded, and his hand ached from holding on to Marta, he realized in that cold moment that he had no history. No past to call on. No lineage to guide him. He only had the way forward. A bridge. A place of fear.

It bore the name "Hell."

And it truly was where he'd find the dead.

CHAPTER TWENTY

Once they'd established that the police were not following them, and that the running was not necessary, they slowed to give their legs a break. Retracing some of Alex's earlier route, they kept to quieter streets, avoiding main roads because they were more likely to have police patrols. Alex felt so tired that every part of him ached, yet sleep was the last thing on his mind. He was gripped by an overwhelming fear that he was walking toward his doom. And his senses were playing strange tricks on him, hearing things that weren't there, seeing details that could not be real. A small piece of paper fluttered in the corner of his eye, and for a second, Alex saw a creature stalking. A car's tires ran over a speed bump in the distance, and Alex thought it was a man's groan that he heard.

And then there was the scent.

He could smell it in the air, faint at first, but growing stronger as they neared the bridge. His mind began to form an image, one that he did not like. This mixture of perspiration and deodorant and musty clothes was so familiar. It was an animal smell, meaty and sweet, unpleasant and attractive at the same time. He'd smelled it once before, in the cemetery when the Jockey had grabbed him.

He didn't say anything to Marta about it. She'd say he was imagining it, or that it was just a product of a tired and over-worked mind, but he knew it was real. The hunter instinct told him that the Jockey was near, stalking him, waiting for his moment. Alex turned to look over his shoulder every now and then, but the streets were empty.

"What's up?" said Marta, her eyes dark with fatigue.

"Nothing," said Alex.

"Then what are you looking at?"

"Nothing."

Marta pulled a mobile phone from her pocket. "I've got Dad's phone," she said. "So we can call an ambulance if we need to . . ."

"Okay," said Alex.

He caught another movement out of the corner of his eye, and wheeled around to see that this time there was no phantom in the shadows. Three boys were sitting on a chain fence across the street, older, bigger, and obviously interested in Marta's phone.

"Put it away," hissed Alex, looking straight ahead.

He'd just managed to catch sight of them standing and knew that they weren't stretching their legs.

"Marta, we have to run again . . ."

"Oh, Alex . . . Why?"

"Don't be scared," he said. "Run!"

Once again they found themselves hurtling through the night, danger behind them, danger ahead. It seemed to Alex that they were being pushed into a corner, one he wasn't sure he could back out of. After a few blocks of sprinting they slowed, and Alex glanced back over his shoulder. There was no one behind them. Perhaps the three shadowy boys never gave chase, or perhaps they ran out of breath. Either way, Alex was convinced they weren't being followed. He stopped, and Marta pulled up beside him, wheezing. They both squatted against a wall, catching their breath. The city streets were getting more dangerous by the hour. The sooner they got to the bridge the better.

He could hear Marta muttering beside him again, communicating with the dark night sky above.

"Does that really help?" he asked.

"You want to give it a try?"

He laughed. "No thanks. Not me . . ."

Marta shrugged. "Okay. It could give you some . . . you know . . . I mean, courage and all that?"

He looked at her. She had been so strong back at the grandstand. Was that courage? Was facing the old man courage? Hitting him? Standing up to danger? Whatever this night was supposed to be, he'd responded to the challenge, found courage, but it had come at a great price. He wondered where the Jockey got his strength from. The brothers? No, the Jockey might have talked tough about brothers and belonging, but really he belonged to no one and nothing. Alex shivered.

He stood, and Marta followed. Alex grinned at her. "You know who you reminded me of back at the grandstand?" he said.

Marta blushed, obviously guessing.

"Even you have a bit of the Jockey in you," he said. "But you've got heaps more . . . I dunno . . . truth in you, or something." Now he blushed, then muttered, "That'll be enough to give me courage for now."

He looked down the road, and the awful weight of his destination dragged him down again. Maybe courage was the strength to put one foot after another. To do the right thing. Or was it simply the ability to care about an old man lying crumpled and broken in the dark night ahead of them?

"Let's go," he said.

And so they walked, the sound of the freeway growing stronger, humming with a life of its own. Alex remembered how the roar of that traffic echoed throughout the incident with the old man. It had been like a crazy sound track to a movie. And now, hearing it again, he thought it might make him nuts. He needed Marta's voice to keep him grounded, stop him from running again, so he started up an aimless conversation in a chirpy voice.

"Where ya been all week?"

"Sick," muttered Marta.

"Taking time off school, eh?"

"I don't want to . . . Sorry, I can't just chat . . . not now . . ."

"Come on, Marta. . . ."

But she was silent, leaving him to the traffic and the memories. He bumped into her a few times, tried to be playful, but she was resolute, not rising to any of his games. Then, finally she spoke, but her words only added to the madness.

"Alex," she said. "What if . . . you know. Have you thought about what it'll be like if we do . . . find the old man?"

"What?" he said, irritated. Why couldn't she just chat about the stars or the weather, anything but this? Had he thought about it? Of course he had. It had been the one thought that had ripped at his mind all the way. Oh yes, he could see the old man, every macabre detail. He shuddered. "I don't know if I can . . . you know . . . If we see him, if I can look . . ."

"But, we might have to move him or touch him."

"Jeezus, Marta. I know that. Can we drop this subject?"

"No. I mean, why is it so scary?" asked Marta. "A dead . . . a body. It's just a human being, same as anyone you'd meet, only they're . . . they're . . ."

"What? Sleeping? Is that what they tell you in church?"

Marta laughed. "Get over it," she said. "No, they do not say dead people are sleeping."

"Let me guess, then," said Alex. "Their souls have gone to heaven."

Marta didn't answer, which was confirmation enough for Alex.

"Must be crowded up there."

"Okay, Mr. Smarty, where do you think their souls have gone, then?"

Alex did not want to think about the answer to that question. He remembered old Alfie's ghoulish story about the shivering ghosts whose souls were rotting in hell. Surely if there was a heaven, then there was also a burning inferno. And if good people went to the first, then bad people wound up in the other.

"It's just crap," he said, swinging punches at spiritual concepts. "Like, if we all had souls, then we'd all know how to treat each other properly, right? Like you've got a soul, and I've got a soul, so they look at each other and say, 'Hey, we souls have to stick together,' and they make the body act right and be a good person because souls have to look after one another. Only, it doesn't ever happen that way, because we do our best to make everyone feel miserable and stuff."

"Not always. Lots of people are good to one another the way you just described. It's only some who . . . who . . ."

"What? Who murder people?"

"Why did you have to say that, Alex?"

He shrugged, wishing he could block this damned traffic noise out of his brain. A bleak cloud descended over his mood, and he walked on quietly, hanging his head, conversation over. The large dark shape of the bridge loomed ahead. What good was his soul to him now? He touched his chest where his heart was, then scratched vigorously, pretending to be terribly itchy. Marta gave him a quick glance.

"Hey," she said, touching his arm.

For a brief second he felt a warmth, then he looked up at the pylon, still a few hundred yards away, but now a massive presence. "That's where we climbed up."

The pylon was like a monster, towering above their heads. Alex looked over at the next pylon, where the old man's hideout had been. There was no light above, no candle burning. When the old man fell, he would have landed at the bottom, only *inside* the pylon. He pointed to it, then whispered, "And that's where he fell."

Marta stared at the base of the pylon, licking her lips. "Then we have to go there," she said, her voice almost lost in the traffic roar.

Alex nodded. Yes, they would have to go there. He willed himself to move forward, fighting against his instinct, which told him to make excuses, find reasons, get the hell out of there now! The ground was uneven under their feet, and they stumbled in the dark, keeping the monolith of the pylon in their sights.

Flashes of the night came to him as he walked. The old man speaking in the darkness in the cemetery. His anger there. The long crawl over the barbed wire. Old Uncle at the tea urn saying they belonged to the same tribe. The Jockey's smile at the police station. The way he'd pulled Alex out of that hole when he'd wanted to go down and see if the old man was still alive.

There was something he'd missed in all this. Some vital clue, but he could not figure it out. All he knew was that his heart was now racing faster, a panic building inside him. He felt the sudden need to get to the bridge fast, to put an end to this monstrous waiting, so he increased the pace. After awhile he heard Marta calling to him from behind.

"Wait up."

"No!" he shouted.

"Alex."

He stopped and turned to her. "What? What do you want? I don't want to wait up. . . . It's me who did this. Don't you get it? It's me who'll get into trouble!"

Marta had reached him by now, and she grabbed him hard by the arm. "Don't you dare say that again!" she yelled.

Alex blinked at her. But it was true, wasn't it? He was in this alone. He'd crawled over sharp steel to go into Hell, and he'd have to do it again.

"I came here," said Marta. "I could run away and say it's all your problem, but it doesn't work like that. So wake up, thickhead. I'm here!"

Alex pulled his arm free. "There's something you don't know," said Alex.

"What?"

"Something . . . stuff that if you knew . . . I don't think you'd want to come with me."

Marta stared at him, and he could see the fear in her eyes. Could taste it in his own mouth. He wanted to confess everything to her, come clean. Perhaps to clear his conscience, or perhaps to test the depth of her friendship.

"Up in the bridge," he said. "When the old man fell . . . I went crazy, Marta. I lost it. I hit him again and again until he was really angry with me. Then I called him names. . . . I made him mad. It was over, but I kept it going."

He looked at her in the eye, challenged her. Now that she knew, surely she'd turn and walk away from him. Leave for good this time. He was a lowlife. A scum kid who tried to be tough and caused the death of an old man instead.

"It doesn't matter," said Marta, so soft he barely heard her.

"But it does . . ."

"Alex! Stop it!" Now she was loud. "What matters is that you're doing the right thing now, doesn't it?"

He wanted to argue, to prove her wrong, but there was nothing left in him to fight with. He couldn't say who was right or who was wrong. Instead, he looked at *that place*. It seemed to be the only thing that made sense at the moment.

"Come on, then," he said.

It took them several minutes to walk all the way around the base of the pylon, stumbling in the dark, the cold gray concrete wall curving around slowly. There was no ladder on this pylon, no access to the bridge above. After several minutes of searching, they did not find a doorway or opening or cut or any access into the concrete structure. Which didn't make sense. If the whole structure was hollow, which it had to be for the old man to fall down the middle of it, why wasn't there a doorway at the bottom? Why have the hole at the top? Unless it was hollow to save on concrete.

"Is there another way in?" asked Marta.

Alex shrugged. "Up the other pylon, I suppose. But that'll just take you to the hole in the old man's hideout. It's dark, we won't be able to see down there."

"Maybe there's a ladder inside the pylon," said Marta.

Alex nodded, heading for the first pylon without a word. That would have to be it. There was a ladder from inside the old man's hideout, which meant a long climb down into the darkness to find . . .

He felt sick and stopped to clutch his stomach, but nothing more came of it. Marta rubbed his back, her nose screwed up, expecting him to release something disgusting at any second. He stood eventually, and shook her hand away. Even though she was comforting him, he felt like she was pushing him on, making him go up to that hideout and down that horrible black hole.

When they arrived at the first pylon, Alex looked at the metal ladder, remembering the struggle to get past the barbed wire to the gap. He doubted if Marta would be able to climb onto the top of the barrier, which meant she'd have to wait below. He didn't know if he could go up there alone, and felt like crying with frustration, when Marta suddenly started climbing up the ladder.

"You can't get through that way," he said. "It's locked . . ."

His words died on his lips as Marta opened the wooden door in the platform and shuffled through to the rest of the wire-enclosed ladder.

"How'd you do that?" he asked.

"I don't know," she said. "Maybe you only thought it was locked."

Alex entered the wire enclosure and started to climb the metal ladder. It seemed much farther up this time, maybe because Marta was slow, pausing every now and then to catch her breath. This painful progress gave Alex too much time to think. He imagined climbing down the hole, finding something in the pitch blackness, crying out at the horror of it. He looked out across the wasteland to see if they were being followed. There was nobody below.

Their progress along the gantry was even slower than the climb up the ladder had been. Marta was obviously frightened by heights, and she had to stop every now and then to will herself forward. Alex spoke comforting words, reassuring her that she'd be okay. Eventually they made it to the hideout and stumbled into the darkness.

"Careful," said Alex, pushing past her. "The hole isn't far away."

He got down onto his knees and scratched around, finding the candle quickly. Now he needed matches. They proved more elusive, until his hand landed on a familiar shape. It was the Jockey's book of matches. There was one match left. Alex tore it free and lit it, squinting at the sudden light. Then he put the flame to the candlewick. A small, warm glow illuminated the hideout. Alex gave a gasp. Everything had changed. Many of the boxes containing the electrical goods had gone. Only about a quarter of their quantity were left, scattered about as if they were dropped in a hurry. One box lay at his feet, and Alex stooped to pick it up. It was a brand-new iron. What had happened to all the other boxes? Had the Jockey come back to claim them?

"There's the hole," said Marta.

Alex walked over and peered into it, but the candle was unable to shine enough light for him to see very far. What it did show was a metal ladder, just as Marta had predicted. Now he would have to make the climb. He handed her the candle and said, "You wait here."

"But, you'll need this," she said. "To see."

"How am I gonna climb then?" he asked.

"Oh," she said, then she smiled, trying to cheer him but only making it worse. "Good luck," she added.

Alex nodded and started to back his way down the ladder, his heart thumping with each passing second. Down there was the darkest place he had ever been to in his life.

"Keep watch," he said to Marta, afraid that whoever took the electrical goods might come back.

She nodded and left the candle by the hole to watch the gantry through the doorway. Alex felt for each rung below him, slowly, making sure he had a strong foothold before he went farther. He didn't want to fall because of a rusty rung. He had gone down far enough for his head to be well below the level of the surface, when he heard Marta cry out.

"Alex! He's coming!"

The Jockey. How stupid had they been? He scrambled to climb back up the ladder, imagining Marta struggling with his brutal teacher, being beaten, pushed, hurt. He pounced on rungs that should have been there, but he was too fast in the darkness. His hand missed first, and then when he scrambled for another grip his foot slipped from the only rung that was holding him up. There was a brief millisecond when he hung in the air, aware of the fate that waited for him, then he fell.

CHAPTER TWENTY-ONE

Marta could see the Jockey slowly advancing along the gantry from her vantage point. He was taking his time, no urgency about him, so maybe he didn't realize that they were inside. She called once again to Alex, not daring to shout. He didn't respond, so she crawled to the edge of the hole, candle held before her, and tried to peer down into the deep nothingness. Once again, the candle offered little assistance.

"Alex? Alex?"

Marta leaned over some more, bracing herself for balance, and dropped the candle by accident in the same gesture. It fluttered briefly, then blew out, snapping the room into darkness.

"Shivers!" hissed Marta.

She crawled back to the entrance of the hideout, watching the Jockey's slow advance. Now what should she do? He'd be here any second, and he probably had a flashlight or matches to light up the room. Then he'd find her. This couldn't get worse, could it?

It was just as she was going through all these possibilities in her mind that the mobile phone started to ring in her pocket, its shrill tones echoing around the room.

"No! No!"

Marta scrambled to remove the phone, dropping it on the concrete floor where it bounced about, playing the ridiculous tune she'd programmed into it another lifetime ago. Luckily the mobile's screen lit up a bright amber, so she could grab it quickly and press the off button. A brief image of her mom or dad on the other end of the line flashed through her mind. She shut that out, sneaking a look at the Jockey, who was running now along the gantry, alerted to her presence by the phone's loud ring.

Marta felt like crying. She was trapped by this vicious, violent monster. She shook her head. No! She was *not* going to let him hurt her. There was another way out. Crawling backward toward the hole, she found its edge with her legs and began to slide into the darkness. Where was that ladder? She should be feeling it by now. She swung her legs around, kicking left and right until at last her foot touched a rung. Taking a firm foothold on the ladder, Marta began to climb down the long drop into the middle of the pylon, when a hand grabbed her by the ankle.

She screamed.

"Will you shut up!" hissed Alex.

"What are you doing? The Jockey . . ."

"Jump!" ordered Alex.

"Jump? Are you . . ."

"Jump! Now!"

He gave an almighty yank on her ankle, and Marta pulled away from the ladder, images of her family flashing through her mind as she fell, praying that she wouldn't be hurt too badly when she hit the . . .

She landed on something soft. Already? That hadn't been far at all. Certainly not the fifty-or-so-yard drop of the entire pylon.

"It doesn't drop all the way," whispered Alex, grabbing her by the arm. "Let's go. Now!"

She was pulled once again, dragged in the darkness. A door opened beside her, and pale light flooded into the small enclosure. Marta just had enough time to see that they were standing in a perfectly round concrete room, cut out of the center of the pylon. The metal ladder was on the wall beside her head, and she could see that her fall had been no more than 15 feet. A mattress was on the floor at her feet, the soft cushion that she'd landed on. There was no time to ask why the mattress was there, or why the hole didn't go all the way down to the bottom of the pylon, Alex was pushing her out onto another gantry. He emerged behind her, then turned to close the door shut as a weight crashed against it from inside the pylon.

The Jockey.

"Quick! Help me!" yelled Alex.

Marta added her weight to Alex's, pushing the door against the Jockey's repeated crashes. As strong as he was, his attacks couldn't budge the door more than a few inches. He was the Jockey, deadly but lightweight, and they had mass on their side.

"Come on, little bro," came the Jockey's muffled voice from inside the pylon. "I just wanna talk . . ."

"Forget it!" shouted Alex.

"Who you got there with you?" shouted the Jockey. "That stupid church girl?"

"Shut up!" shouted Marta, incensed by the taunt.

"What are you hanging with her for?" called the Jockey, repeatedly bashing the door. "She's a loser. You wanna be a loser, too? She's an ugly nobody. Everyone hates her. They laugh at her more than they laugh at you. . . ."

Alex's face turned a hard set of determination. He glanced at Marta to see if she'd been stung by the Jockey's words, but she was too busy holding him out. They couldn't keep this up forever, sooner or later he'd push through. Looking around desperately for anything that might keep this door closed, Alex saw a small wooden wedge on the gantry. It was probably used to hold the door open when the workers came through, but it could also wedge the door shut long enough for them to escape.

"Keep pushing," he whispered to Marta, indicating the wedge on the ground with his eyes.

She nodded, understanding his intentions. Alex squatted to grab the wedge, taking some of his weight from the door. It pushed open a few inches, knocking Alex sideways. His fingers clipped the wedge, sending it spinning toward the edge of the gantry.

"No!" he shouted, falling forward and grabbing the wedge by his fingertips before it rolled over the edge. The door was flying against him now, bashing his rib cage, and Alex got back up on his knees, pushing his shoulder against the metal.

"We've gotta close it!" he shouted.

"Okay!" yelled Marta, her face red with the strain.

"Alex," called the Jockey. "Now you're really pissing me off. Come on, we gotta talk, man . . ."

They both pushed as hard as they could, their feet scrabbling on the metal floor of the gantry for a grip, their faces wet with sweat. The Jockey was swearing loudly on the other side, calling them disgusting, vile names. All their effort was on one single thought. Eventually they had the door almost shut, and Alex waited for a pause between the Jockey's heaving pushes, then shoved the wedge in under the door. He kicked it hard with his foot, again and again, until it seemed to hold the door in place.

"Go!" he shouted.

Marta turned on the gantry and ran, Alex behind her. There was only a short stretch of walkway on this side before they came to another ladder, leading up to the bridge's apron. With the metal door booming behind them from the Jockey's repeated crashes, they climbed as fast as they could up the ladder. Alex could hear Marta wheezing with the effort, and he hoped she'd be able to make it. At the top of the ladder, through a short dark tunnel in the apron, was an access cover. Alex shouted for Marta to push it open. She did so, and they crawled up into a small, concrete storage room, not much bigger than the hideout had been. There were heavy wooden booms lying along the floor, the type used to form roadblocks. Other equipment was stacked up in boxes around the room, obviously waiting to be used by the maintenance crews that serviced the bridge. The room had a window with a wire screen over it and a door that was locked. Alex slid the cover back over the access hole.

"He'll get through any second," he said through panting breath.

Marta nodded, so exhausted she was unable to speak. Alex dragged one of the wooden booms across the access cover, then another and another. Once again it wouldn't stop the Jockey completely, but it would slow him down. Now they had to figure out how to get out of the maintenance room. Alex rattled the window repeatedly, but the wire screen held firm. Marta started rummaging around in the toolboxes stacked up against the wall and came out with an electric power tool.

"What's that?" said Alex.

"Angle grinder," muttered Marta, looking around the room.

"How do you know tha . . ."

"Sh," she said. She pulled another toolbox away and found what she was after, the power outlet socket. The cord just reached, and Marta turned to the window, telling Alex to shield his eyes.

"There's going to be lots of sparks, okay?"

"What about you?"

Marta shrugged and glanced down at the access hole. "We've got to get out of here."

She switched the power tool on and an almighty screech filled the room. Alex blocked his ears, watching as Marta cut the wire with the angle grinder. Sparks flew in a beautiful display of reds, yellows, and oranges. Luckily, most fell downward, bouncing off Marta's jeans. The smell of burning metal was soon mixed with the smell of burning clothes, and Marta switched the machine off, brushing her thighs briskly.

"These were my favorites."

"How come you know how to use one of those?" said Alex, an indignant note in his voice.

"My dad has one, silly. Do you think girls spend their time playing with dolls or something?"

A loud thump hit the access cover below them, and they gave a yelp of fright.

"Come on," said Marta.

Both she and Alex grabbed the wire cover to the window, avoiding the hot edges, and pulled hard. It gave way after a few attempts, and Alex picked up the angle grinder and smashed the glass out of the window with it. He then proceeded to bash all the broken glass along the edges, until they had a relatively safe hole to climb out of. This all took up precious time. Alex looked over at the access hole. The wooden beams had moved considerably. He slid them back over again, then helped boost Marta out of the window.

It took some effort, but she finally made it through, panting as Alex emerged from the maintenance room. They were on the edge of the freeway now, the occasional car flashing past them at frightening speed. Inside the room they could hear the Jockey trying to push the booms off the access hole. There was no time to lose.

"Run!" said Alex, taking hold of his friend's hand.

"You go first," said Marta. "I'll slow you down."

Alex took her hand and squeezed it painfully, a fierce look in his eyes. "If you don't run, then I'm staying here with you, and we face him. I'm not leaving you alone."

Marta smiled at him, her little hero. He stood several inches shorter than her, a little punk looking so tough in the amber light of the freeway.

"Okay," she said. "Let's go."

Then they ran, an unknown destination ahead of them. Behind them in the maintenance room the access cover moved with each thump.

Soon it would be open.

CHAPTER TWENTY-TWO

They were exposed out here on the bridge, easy prey to be picked off by seeing eyes. Alex kept a constant check over his shoulder, watching for the Jockey. Still no sign of him, which meant they had a bit of time to find somewhere to hide and catch their breath. So many thoughts were running through his brain, clashing together, threatening to split his head open. He just wanted to stop and figure it all out. The fall down the pylon, the mattress, the other way out . . . and most importantly, the missing body of the old man. One thing was for certain, unless the guy hit his head going over, he was well and truly alive right now.

The bridge sloped down toward a long flat ribbon of freeway that circled the city to their right. Once they'd made it down this steep incline to flatter ground they could find a place to climb over the side and get back into the darker industrial site area.

The cars still roared past them, and every now and then Alex would catch a startled look from a driver or a passenger, wondering what these two kids were doing out here on the freeway at this time of night. A vague thought came to him that one of these people might call the police from a mobile phone. Would that be a good thing or a bad thing? There was no time to stop and figure it out.

Marta was clutching her chest, and her pace had slowed down considerably. They had to get out of this light. The bridge had almost flattened out by now, and Alex stopped to peer over the side. He could see a spot a bit farther on, about a hundred yards, where a dark hill sloped up to meet the side of the freeway. That was their way out.

"Can you go on a bit more?" he asked Marta, who was leaning against the guardrail as he surveyed the side.

She didn't speak, just nodded her head. Even in this dull light he could see that her face was as pale as death. He took her hand and rubbed it. "Come on, almost there."

And then he headed forward again, keeping Marta in front of him in case she stumbled or collapsed from the effort. His own body was screaming out with pain, begging him to put an end to this torture of running, but he shut it out. They came to the point where the hill rushed up to the freeway, and Alex helped Marta over the metal barrier, giving one last backward glance for their hunter before climbing over himself.

Running, slipping, half sliding, they made it to the bottom of the hill. A vast black expanse stretched out before them, with very few buildings or hiding spots. Alex told Marta to crouch down there and wait while he checked the area out. He backtracked under the bridge to see if the other side offered any better protection. This side was nearer the water, a murky stretch of marshy sludge that gave off a bad smell. An old, large warehouse stood near the water's edge, dilapidated and neglected. The windows were broken, and a wobbly wire fence ran around its perimeter. Alex ran back to Marta to see her bent double, being sick.

"I'm okay," she said between breaths as he approached her. "I'm okay."

She straightened and attempted to smile. Alex smiled back. "Through here," he said, motioning with his head. She followed him, slowly, stumbling across the uncertain terrain toward the foul-smelling water and the unused warehouse. They went at a snail's pace now, with barely a flicker of light to see by. Alex hoped that it would be too dark for the Jockey to spot them, even from the vantage point of the bridge. Eventually they made it to the wire fence that surrounded the warehouse. It had a gate, which stood half broken, swaying on one hinge, and Alex pushed it aside so that Marta could get through.

"Do you think he's still following us?" she said as she shuffled through the narrow gap.

Alex surveyed the bridge, but there was no sign of the Jockey. He could be hiding anywhere, poking his head up to look at them. Their major advantage was that this warehouse was on the other side of the bridge to where the Jockey would be running. He'd have to cross over the freeway to see them.

The huge double doors to the warehouse were completely missing, and they walked in cautiously. Anything, or anyone, could be living in here. The traffic noise was much quieter inside, and their footsteps echoed loudly, announcing their arrival. Alex saw a ladder leading up to an office, and he pointed at it. Marta nodded. They climbed up, slowed by fatigue and caution, reaching the office, which miraculously had a chair. Alex immediately slumped into it, then looked up at Marta, who swayed in the doorway.

"Sorry," he said.

"No, you have it . . ."

"Get in the chair."

She didn't need any more convincing. Alex tried peering out the windows, but they were covered in years of grime and offered nothing. When he turned back to Marta, he saw that she had the mobile phone out.

"What are you doing?" he said.

"They tried to call me, Alex," said Marta. "Before, when . . . When he was coming along the gantry. They're worried. I just want to . . ."

"To tell them where we are," spat Alex.

"No. To tell them we're okay, I guess."

She pressed a button on the phone and it came to life in her hands, the amber screen warm in the cold light of the warehouse. Marta stared at it, muttering under her breath.

"What's up?" asked Alex.

"No signal."

Alex sighed and lay down on the vinyl floor, allowing his body to stop screaming in protest. They were quiet for some time, just breathing. He listened for any strange noises and could hear water dripping from somewhere far off, could hear the distant traffic, muted. Tuning into each sound, Alex let them form pictures in his mind. A faint scrape could have been a shoe on the ground, but he saw a dried leaf blowing against a wall. A scattering noise above could have been fingernails on the floor, but he saw rats running in single file, their noses constantly sniffing out the strange human smell. Alex sniffed, too, scanned the air for the sweet, pungent scent he'd smelled earlier. There was dust, grease, grime, and foul water on the air, but no smell of the Jockey.

He stilled his mind even further, learning to block out unnecessary sounds and smells—Marta's breathing, his own perspiration, his heart still thumping—so he could concentrate. He felt himself floating out of the room, moving right, left, looking for his prey. Rats ran below, pausing on their hind legs to sniff at him. A bird watched him from high above, blinking and indifferent. Insects scuttled beside him, ignoring his presence. On he went, out the doors, sniffing the night air. The wind blew around him, the moon shone in his face, the ground floated like a black river below him. He found nothing.

A voice whispered in his ear. *Alex*, it said. *I'm waiting for you. Are you waiting for me?* It was a familiar voice, one he'd heard many times before. He strained. Who owned this voice? Alex concentrated everything into the one act of listening, until there was nothing but that voice.

Then he knew. The lion.

Alex opened his eyes. Marta was asleep. How much time had passed? She should be home in bed, this wasn't her problem. He'd seen how frightened she was back in the pylon, looking down that hole for him, the candle shaking in her hand. Alex couldn't call out to her, his fall had knocked the wind out of him. All he could do was lie on his back, trying to figure out how he was still alive. Was it a miracle? He'd watched the candle slowly fall onto his body, then Marta disappear. Eventually the pressure in his lungs released, and he was able to sit up. That's when he saw Marta's legs poking over the side of the hole.

What had the Jockey been up to, coming back to the pylon? Did he follow them there? That would explain why he wasn't rushing. Or maybe he didn't know they were in there. Maybe he had other business in that dank room, moving boxes, perhaps? So when he heard Marta's phone ring, he ran because he *knew* there was another exit. Of course! Hadn't he followed them down the so-called empty pylon without hesitation? He said he'd never been inside that room before, but Alex knew that to be a lie now. How many other lies were there?

The old thief.

Was the Jockey in some kind of partnership with him? It would explain a lot. Like how the old man had been able to find Alex so easily in the dark at the cemetery. He was at the right spot because the Jockey had told him to wait there. The stealing of the jacket had been a setup, so had the revenge. The Jockey had almost admitted that when he'd said how things had turned out better than he'd expected.

It had all been a challenge for Alex, a test. But why was the old man in on it? One thing was for certain, no one had expected him to fall down that hole. The Jockey had been genuinely scared then, thinking the old guy might have really hurt himself when he went down. And then, after he'd told Alex to run, he must have gone down to check on his companion. Obviously the thief had survived.

Was it revenge that had motivated the Jockey to engineer all this? A payback for the phone call that evening a long time ago? You hurt me, I hurt you back a hundred times over? But even that didn't make sense. The Jockey was more likely to pound him to pulp for revenge. There had to be something else. All that effort, and for what? He wanted to grab his teacher now, shake him, demand the answer. How dare he use him like this?

He looked at Marta; she was still asleep. The air inside the room was as cold as outside, but somehow it felt stifling to him. He had to go out for a while, so he quietly left her there and climbed back down the ladder to the warehouse floor. He was cautious, even though he felt that he'd checked this area out before. Coming to the entrance, he scanned the wasteland, feeling a strange mix of relief and disappointment that the Jockey was nowhere to be seen.

Alex wished he'd grabbed Marta's mobile phone. He felt the need to talk to his dad, hear his voice. But what would his father say to him? Would he yell? Say he's had Marta's father over, worried sick? Would he tell Alex to come home?

Alex sat on an old box and thought about the way home. It seemed the hardest thing to do, to stand up now and walk the long road back to his house. His whole body felt weary at the thought of it, as if there was an enormous barrier in his way, a thousand weights holding him back. He shivered, but not with the cold this time. How could he go home? So much had changed. Would his father want him back?

Tears came to his eyes, even though he tried to stop them. He heard voices, saw people, but they were ghosts.

He heard his father making that phone call to the police that started the whole madness. And for what? All it did was make the Jockey a thousand times more dangerous.

Now he sobbed, releasing tension and fear.

He could hear his father saying to him, "You have to stand up to people like the Jockey."

His body shook, rattled with a power stronger than anything he could will. So much damage had been done, all because of "the right thing."

"No," he said. "I don't believe in any of that . . ."

He could hear the Jockey, telling him to grab what he could.

"No," he said again.

He searched for his father's voice, for something that would help him, but he could only hear a faint whisper, a rustle against the wind, telling him the sacrifice was worth it.

The sacrifice.

And then his tears ended. He wiped his eyes until his vision was no longer distorted through watery lenses. When he looked up, he saw a figure silhouetted against the glow of the city lights. It was a long distance away, but there was no mistaking its shape.

Alex stood, then moved behind a brick pillar, keeping an eye on the Jockey from his dark vantage point. The Jockey was looking still, searching one way, then the other. Alex watched him carefully, tried to read his thoughts, his emotions. Was he still angry? Still bent on revenge?

There was no way of telling.

And then a dreadful thought came to him.

He could call out. Just shout. The Jockey would be with him in a minute. Then they could put an end to this.

His heart beat with excitement. His mouth tingled. He wanted to do it.

Then he thought of Marta.

Alex watched as the Jockey held something to his face. His hands. A faint voice drifted in on the breeze, washed past him, surging in and out of earshot.

"Alex!"

So quiet.

"Alex!"

Calling for him.

He listened, waited for more words, but they were either swallowed by the wind or never spoken. The Jockey dropped his hands, turned to walk into the darkness. Alex thought that he heard one more sentence carried on the softest of breezes. He watched the figure of the Jockey completely vanish, then went back into the warehouse, those last words still blowing through his mind.

"I'm waiting for you . . ."

CHAPTER TWENTY-THREE

"The Jockey tricked you, Alex. Anyone could see that."

"I know," he said.

They were still in the warehouse office, their sanctuary, continuing an argument that began the minute Alex returned. Marta had wanted to walk to where they'd get a reception on the mobile phone, so she could call her parents and get them to come rescue them. Alex told her to make a call if she wanted to, but he still had unfinished business with the Jockey.

Now she was standing, edgy and angry, pointing at him. "Stop being a total idiot," she said. "You've done your tough guy thing tonight. Just come home now . . ."

Alex shook his head. "I don't expect you to understand . . ." he began.

"You got that right!" shouted Marta. "The one thing I understand is that you're . . . you're so difficult. That you're such a hard person to like."

"Ah, well," shrugged Alex. "At least God still likes me."

"I reckon even He'd have trouble with you," said Marta.

Alex smiled, watching Marta's expression change from fury to remorse in an instant.

"Oh, Alex," she said. "I'm sorry. That was a horrible thing to say."

"Na, you're right," he said. "It's the first bit of truth I've heard all night. Can't you see? That's the whole frigging point, Marta. Everyone thinks I'm crap. My mom married another man so she didn't have to parent me anymore. And even when she has access weekends, she makes excuses. My dad . . . Well, I'm just a disappointment to him, aren't I? The school hates me, the seniors treat me like a punching bag . . ."

"But I don't, Alex. I'm your friend."

"I know," he said quietly. "But you still don't get how he made me feel tonight. Not the lies, I don't mean them. There was other stuff, Marta. The stuff he taught me. I felt tall."

"Well, I wish there wasn't," said Marta, fussing with her jacket, even though it didn't need any attention.

"See," said Alex, smiling at her. "Even you can't like *all* of me."

Marta turned away from him, looking out the broken window into the darkness.

"I have to find out," said Alex. "I have to know if I can keep hold of something from tonight. Maybe I don't have to be a bastard like him. . . . I have to find that out, Marta. I can't let this end with me going home. . . . You go if you want to, that's okay."

"Oh, that's just great," said Marta. "That makes a whole lot of sense."

She walked to the ladder and started climbing down. Alex watched her disappear, then started making the climb himself. He couldn't let her stand outside alone, the Jockey might have doubled back. He would go with her until she made the call, wait until she was safely in the car for home, then he'd finish the night . . . somehow. The only vague idea he had was to track the Jockey down, to turn the tables and become the hunter. But where in the city would he find his prey? Then he remembered the cemetery. Those dwellers there had known the old thief. And the old thief was his only link now to the Jockey.

Marta was outside, hands in her jacket pockets, the mobile phone nowhere to be seen.

"Did you make the call already?" asked Alex.

"No," said Marta.

She started walking across the wasteland, heading back toward the bridge.

"Wait," called Alex, catching up with her. "You'll probably get a reception soon . . ."

"The phone is switched off," said Marta.

"But . . ."

"But what? You thought I was running home? I'm your friend, Alex. Even though you can't see it. And I'll tell you something for nothing, there's plenty of ways to make someone feel tall. You felt tall with the Jockey? Well, it makes me feel like shit that you don't feel tall with me."

Alex nearly fell to the ground. It was the first time in his life he'd heard Marta use a swear word. "Shivers" was about as wild as she ever got. He stood in awe, watching her merge into the darkness, then he shouted, "Wait!" and ran again to catch up.

"You swore," he said.

"Get over it."

"But you, like, never swear."

"And you never think about who your real friends are."

"Okay," he said. "That's me, a total jerk."

Marta stopped walking and turned to him. "You know, after a while that excuse stops being cute."

Once more she left him alone in the dark. He caught up again, but kept his thoughts to himself this time. She stopped walking and turned once again to him, searching his eyes, reaching into him. "Do you remember the first time I started coming to your place after school?" she said, her voice almost inaudible.

Alex nodded. "Yeah," he said.

"It was when the Jockey had been arrested. Well, a few weeks after, anyway. I'd been watching you on the bus ever since they put the Jockey in jail, and you looked so . . . I don't know . . . hurt or something. Then one day I heard about how you'd been taken into the bathroom by the seniors and made to stand in that urinal thing . . ."

"Thanks for reminding me . . ."

"Everyone said you deserved it," said Marta.

"Oh, well, gee. Thanks doubly now," said Alex, a sharp edge of anger to his voice.

"They did. I'm only telling you what happened," said Marta. "They said you'd been so annoying that the seniors had every right to . . . you know. So that's when I came around. I knocked on your door, but you looked really disappointed to see me there. At the time I made up some excuse to get a schoolbook from you, but really I wanted to just see how you were doing. Talk to you. You were pretty rude. Shut the door on me. So I prayed, Alex. I asked for help, and I received an answer. Then I came around again the next day with the chocolate biscuits. You remember that?"

"Yes," said Alex.

"Thought you would. That's when we started hanging out together after school. All that time we spent together, all the stuff we said to each other . . . What kept you there? Was it the chocolate biscuits I brought over each day?"

Alex laughed. "Give me a break," he said. "Whatya take me for? Some kind of shallow jerk or something?"

"No," said Marta quietly. "I don't. But sometimes you're so anxious to be tough or whatever, that you're too stupid to see the obvious."

She smiled at him, the old Marta, then kept walking. As Alex caught up, he felt that he wasn't chasing her anymore, but walking side by side, continuing with something that began so many nights ago in the conversation they'd had after school where he told Marta about his father's phone call to the police. He'd never wondered before why she was the only person he'd talked to about it, but now he thought he knew. Marta was rock solid as a friend. She might get angry, she might even swear once every decade, but she would stick with him for as long as her courage held out.

And he'd been too dumb to see that.

He placed his hand on her shoulder and gave her a gentle shove.

"Hey!" she said. "I nearly fell over."

"I was just thinking," he said.

"That'd be a new experience."

"Exactly. I was thinking that I'm so dumb, I look in a mirror to see if my eyes are open."

He heard the satisfying sound of Marta chuckling beside him. "I haven't heard that one before," she said.

"It's new. Your turn."

"Okay," she said. "Um, you're so dumb, your dog teaches *you* tricks."

"All right," said Alex, warming to the task. "I'm so dumb, I take a ruler to bed to see how long I slept."

Marta groaned. "Oh, that is so bad. You're so dumb, you don't know how to use an angle grinder."

"Hey, that's not fair."

"Well," said Marta. "I thought all boys knew stuff like that. After all, isn't that what being a man is?"

"Can I help it if you're a New-Age feminist chick?"

They continued in this way, insulting, joking, slinging verbal snowballs that hit and bounced and missed their mark. It was a way of warding off the night.

And it was a way of avoiding where they both knew they were headed. Back into the city. Back to the Jockey.

CHAPTER TWENTY-FOUR

The jokes had dried up, the lightness gone, and now all they had was nausea, aching muscles, and headaches from lack of sleep as they made the endless trek back into the city. Every step they took they questioned in their minds what madness had led them to keep going when they could be back at home in their beds.

Alex clung to his germ of an idea, not allowing it to grow weaker and dimmer with each passing stretch of cold, damp road. Those people who'd sat around the campfire at the cemetery would have to know something about the old thief. He was certain that the hideout up on the bridge was more a storage area for stolen goods, and not the old thief's real home. Look at how quickly they cleaned the place out. There'd only been a cruddy mattress and a wooden box for furniture. Something told him that the thief would have stolen much better for himself.

No, there had to be somewhere else that he'd find them. And

when he did, he'd walk in with the element of surprise and . . . and . . . do what? Try as he might, Alex couldn't come up with any more to his plan. He thought about the possibilities, but his imagination didn't go any further than simply finding the Jockey and the thief together. What good was that going to do him? He smiled grimly, remembering his "dumb" jokes with Marta. Even they had a ring of truth to them.

Alex knew the score. He might not be able to read books all that well, but he could read the looks on his teachers' faces, the frustration, the resignation. He spent too much of his life screwing around and doing useless things. He couldn't concentrate for more than a few minutes without his head spinning off on one crazy thought or another. How the hell was he going to outsmart the Jockey?

He looked at Marta, walking with her head bowed low, shivering in the cold. She had a thick jacket on and she was freezing. A sudden wave of protectiveness came over him. He wanted to take her home, put her back in the world where she belonged. Her mother and father would be so worried about her. Then he thought of his own dad, and felt a horrible, empty pit of sadness. He went over to the cars parked by the road and ran his fingers along their dewy bodies, making a thin wobbly line. He had the urge to write his name, but thought that would just be another dumb thing to do.

"We're here," said Marta.

Alex looked up to be confronted by a classic image from a horror movie: huge, wrought-iron gates framed by a cloudy, moonlit sky. They'd arrived at the cemetery. This was a far better way of getting inside than scrambling over the wall and running into a night visitor. A long white gravel path stretched away from them, branching out into three different directions farther on. One of these paths would lead them to the campers.

"Which way?" asked Marta.

Alex pointed to the middle path confidently. It seemed the best bet.

"Are you sure?" asked Marta.

"Trust me," said Alex, setting off. "I have this, like, amazing sense of direction."

The gravel crunched under their feet, making a comforting noise that seemed to lift their spirits. Gravestones lined their way, large, small, broken, well-kept. Some had deep, dark shadows with strange, irregular shapes. Was that a hand or a tree branch? And there. Did that shape move?

Alex looked over at Marta and said, "Spooky, huh?"

"No, not really," she said.

Even so, he caught her looking from side to side and knew that she, too, was wondering about things lurking in the shadows. They passed a large gray headstone, and Marta stopped to read the inscription in the pale glimmer from a nearby streetlight.

"Alex, look at this. *Here lies Mary Goodnough.* She was only six."

He grunted, looking this way and that for the campfire. A sudden restlessness had come over him, an urgency to keep moving, get the night over with. "Let's go . . ."

Marta shook her head absently, still reading the inscription. "There's a poem, too. *This lovely child so young and fair/ Called hence by early doom/ Just came to show how sweet a flower/ In Paradise could bloom.*"

An awful shadow descended on Alex as Marta read the poem, as if each word, each line, was drawing him closer to a cold, lonely place. His heart started to beat faster, and he dug his heels into the gravel, anchoring himself to the spot. This was no fear of the unknown that he felt, no spooking at shadows in the dark. This was fear of an all too familiar place. An emptiness that he ran from each and every day.

"So beautiful," whispered Marta.

Alex kicked his foot into the ground, and a spray of gravel bounced off a gravestone opposite.

"Come on," he said, then started walking.

Marta caught up, a puzzled expression on her face. "Alex?" she said.

"Leave it."

"But . . ."

"Do you think she's listening, Marta? The little kid? Maybe she's sitting over there on the gravestone . . ."

"Stop it."

"Look! I can see her. She's whispering to you . . . 'Father, it's so cold in here. Mother, it's so dark.' "

He lunged at her suddenly. "There she is!"

Marta squealed, and Alex bent double, laughing so much he didn't even feel her punch him on the arm.

"Idiot!" she said, standing away from him, arms crossed.

He stood, wiping his eyes. "I thought you didn't believe in ghosts?"

"I don't."

"Oh no. Of course not."

"I believe in our spirits," she said. "I believe that the spirits of those who have gone do come back, to . . . you know . . ."

"To what? Spook us?"

"No, silly. To help us out."

He felt a brief cold tingle and remembered something his

mother used to say about shivers being the result of someone walking across your grave.

Marta had obviously noticed his shiver. "What's the matter?" she said, a half smile on her face. "Seen a ghost?"

"Not scared," he said.

She looked around the cemetery, wild-eyed, then smiled at him. "The spirits sometimes get restless, you know," she said. "They call to our spirits. 'Come and play,' they say, at night when we're sleeping."

"Oh, sure."

"And sometimes our spirits go with them, play these wild games where only the dead walk. Sometimes our spirits can't ever get back . . ."

"Still not scaring me," said Alex, but his voice was uncertain.

"So they try to enter the wrong body . . ."

"Sure, sure . . ."

Suddenly a faint quivering finger tickled Alex on the back of his neck, and he swung around, but there was nothing there. "Stop it," he said. But the finger tickled him again, and he swung around once more, remembering the old man in the dark. Now the finger crawled from his neck up his scalp, and Alex shouted with fear, dancing on the spot, brushing his head with his hands.

"What is it?" said Marta.

Alex couldn't answer. He brushed and brushed at his head, until it was raw and aching, only stopping when he was satisfied that the sensation of the fingers had gone. Then he turned to Marta accusingly and said, "What did you do?"

"Nothing . . ."

"But you must have . . ."

"It was probably a spider or something."

"Yeah," said Alex, rubbing his head one last time. "Probably."

They continued down the path, and Alex glanced over at his friend. He couldn't be sure, but he thought he saw a faint smile on her lips. It was too dark to tell.

The cold seemed to have intensified since they entered the cemetery, and they thrust their hands into their pockets. After a while they slowed down, each aware that they hadn't come across any campfire or sign of life yet. Alex searched through the headstones for the fire but saw nothing. No doubt it had burned down by now, and all the occupants were sleeping. He stopped and closed his eyes, trying to remember which way he and the Jockey had walked when they'd left the cemetery. Marta waited beside him, shuffling to keep warm. After a minute she spoke.

"Okay, Mr. Sense-of-direction. Where are they?"

"I'm thinking."

They were at a crossroad in the paths and had three more directions to choose from. Alex contemplated playing "eeny, meeny, miney, mo," but he thought this would not go down too well with Marta. The camp had been roughly in the center of the cemetery, so the path straight ahead was probably the best bet.

"This way," he said, sounding a little less certain of the direction.

They headed off, with Alex scanning left and right for even the merest glow. Marta glanced at him, a worried look on her face. Suddenly he felt the responsibility of his role. He was the leader, taking her into dangerous territory. She relied on him in this moment, and he did not want to let her down. He willed the fire to come, calling upon anyone who would listen to guide his feet in the right direction. . . .

"There it is," said Marta.

"Where?" said Alex.

"There. That's the campfire . . . I think."

It was off to their right, a soft red glow of embers they could see beyond a stand of trees.

"Let's go," said Alex.

"But we have to walk across people's graves," said Marta.

He paused, remembering the strange tickling fingers on the back of his neck. "Are you sure you didn't do anything to me back there?" he asked.

"Alex, I didn't," said Marta.

He searched her eyes, then nodded, looking across the graves they would have to step over. "Okay," he said. "We'll just have to . . . um . . . say 'sorry' or something."

Marta nodded, and they began scrambling across the graves, both whispering a hasty apology as they jumped, stood, stumbled, and stomped over the resting place of the dead. At last they came to the edge of the clearing, arriving on the opposite side to where he and the Jockey had emerged earlier that night. He could see the dark clump of trees on the other side of the clearing, and he gave a little shiver, remembering his encounter in there.

As he'd predicted, the occupants of the campfire were all asleep. Alfie, the old man with the carriage and the shivering ghost story, was no longer there, but the couple were curled up under their blanket, wrapped in each other's arms for warmth. The two young men slept with their backs to the fire, each covered in an old army blanket. It looked like a cold place to spend the night.

"What do we do now?" whispered Marta.

"Don't know," replied Alex.

He didn't want to wake them, yet the whole idea of coming here was to ask them about the thief and the Jockey. They could wait until dawn, but somehow he knew that the morning light would bring an end to his adventure. Just the reality of daylight, an ordinary city, would break whatever strange spell held them to the night.

Marta crouched near the fire, and Alex joined her, holding his hands out for warmth.

"My nose is dripping," whispered Marta.

"Mine, too. God, it's so cold . . ."

Another voice spoke, deep and withdrawn behind layers of clothing and blanket. "Get the hell away from our fire before I break your fingers."

Alex stood, startled, Marta beside him.

"Sorry," he said. "We're only . . . we're . . ."

The young man under the blanket closest to him sat up, rubbing his head, peering at them.

"What do you two kids want? Go home to frigging bed."

"We're looking for someone. . . ."

The man's companion woke, sitting up, an angry look on his face. Alex remembered that he was the one who'd given the old thief a sharp kick when he was down. He looked like he had a wild temper.

"Who the hell are you?" he snapped.

"I'm Alex," he said, knowing that it was a stupid answer, but unable to think of anything else.

"So?"

"There was an old man here," Alex said, quickly before they ran them out of the cemetery. "Before. He stole my jacket. You chased him . . ."

"You know him?" said the snarly young man.

Alex took a quick breath. Had to speak fast here, get the message across. "No. He robbed me, and I wanna get him back, only I don't know where to find him. . . ."

"Robbed you?" said the first man, looking suspicious now.

"Yes," said Alex.

"Then how come you're wearing a jacket?" asked Snarly.

Alex froze. Damn! Now what did he say? Any excuse would sound weak.

"It's my little brother's jacket," said Marta, lying so convincingly that Alex could almost see her fictional little brother in his imagination. So much for Marta's devotion to the truth. She sounded like a natural.

"Yeah," added Alex, taking back the initiative. "So, I'm after this guy, and I know you chased him before, but I wanna know where he lives. . . ."

"You think we hang out with thieves, do ya?" said the snarly one, a hard look in his eyes.

"No, I never said . . ."

"You think because we sleep out here we're some kind of scum, eh? Some kind of deadheads who steal stuff?"

"We don't think that," said Marta. "We're trying to find the man . . ."

"I've got a job, you know that?" said Snarly, warming up to the fight, now. "That's shocked ya, eh? I got a job. And him over there, he gets work, too. We're not losers. Just because we sleep out here."

"I know," said Alex, although in truth he was surprised to hear that the men had jobs and a life outside of sleeping under the sky by a dying fire.

"You're a little snot," said Snarly. "Isn't he, John? He's a little snot."

His mate nodded. "Yeah, he's a little snot all right. Thinks he's some kind of know-it-all, I bet."

They were just getting settled into their character analysis of Alex when another voice spoke from under a blanket, a girl's voice, and she sounded none too pleased.

"Hey!" she yelled. "I'm trying to frigging sleep here. Just tell the little punk what he wants so youse can all shut the hell up!"

"Go back to sleep," said Snarly, but the girl was wide awake now, sitting up with the blanket pulled around her. Her boyfriend groaned beside her, then snuggled up closer.

"Hey, you," shouted the girl, pointing to Alex. "Do I come into your bedroom at night and wake you up?"

"Um . . . no," said Alex.

"Then why the hell are you in mine? Eh? Get outa here. This is my place, and I wanna sleep."

She lay back under the blanket, closing her eyes. To Alex's dismay, the other two men copied her, muttering about "stuck-up little snots," curling under their blankets to sleep.

"Aren't you gonna tell us?" said Alex.

"Jeezus!" shouted the woman. "He hangs around the dam. Now clear off before I smack your stupid faces. I'm trying to sleep!"

She was making more noise than the lot of them put together, and had probably woken the dead in their graves, but nevertheless she'd told them what they'd come for. Alex tapped Marta on the shoulder, and they walked quickly back down the path.

"Where's the dam?" asked Marta.

"The river," said Alex. "You know, past the picnic area where they have all them fireworks shows and stuff. It's another long walk . . ."

Marta groaned, saying she wished she were fitter.

"You could always go back," said Alex.

"No," said Marta, sounding less convincing. Then she turned to him and said, "Why don't you come back?"

Alex shook his head and kept walking, not slowing his pace for her. Marta ran to catch up with him, her hands thrust defiantly into her pockets, her face staring once again at the ground. After a few moments of walking, Alex heard Marta muttering under her breath, and he strained to hear what she was saying.

"Not another prayer!" he snapped. "Is it for me?"

"It does work, you know," said Marta. "There's stories in the Bible, and stories I hear at church about, you know, members of the congregation. It makes things better for them."

"Why can't I have a normal friend," said Alex, rolling his eyes.

"I am normal, thank you."

"You pray to someone you've never met. You believe in stories about miracles and stuff that supposedly happened thousands of years ago. . . . It's just mumbo jumbo."

To his surprise, Marta laughed. "You should talk," she said. "Going off into the 'wilderness' to be a man. Acting like you're some kind of member of a tribe or something."

"It wasn't my idea. . . . It was the Jockey's."

"Yeah," snorted Marta. "That'd be right. Trust him to get it all wrong."

"How do you mean?"

"I did that assignment last term, Alex. Those boys in the tribe in your book. When they go out, it's not just about killing something. I bet the Jockey never even read that book. The hunt they go on, it's about their courage and their tribe and their ancient ancestors. . . . It's about becoming better men. The ancient spirits guide the young hunter."

He stared at her, wanting to knock her argument down, but he remembered the storyteller calling the ancient warriors.

"So what?" he said, trying to dismiss her argument. So what if there were long lines of dead men, or ancestors, guiding what happened? What would the Jockey's ancestors look like? Criminals in prison clothes? Bandits in corny masks? Puny runts with broken noses? He laughed at the thought of them, refusing to tell Marta what was so funny when she asked.

They continued along the cemetery path, and after awhile Marta started praying under her breath again. Alex tried to drown out the noise by singing a mock hymn, full of irreverent words and decidedly anti-Christian sentiments. "God's on the toilet, pushing out a prayer, and Jesus he's outside with his nose in the air . . ." So Marta prayed louder, her voice straining to drown him out, until they created a cacophony of noise.

He couldn't keep the mockery up, and eventually he fell silent. He was relieved to hear that she, too, had gone quiet. But even in this empty space there was no relief. Marta's words about the ancestors came back to him, and he remembered something, a small memory: his old Poppa sitting in the backyard one sunny afternoon not long before he died. The old man's face, stubbly and dark with too much sun and grime. He seemed still, peaceful even, but his expression was so sad. Alex remembered the exact seconds of walking out to the clothesline and seeing the old man this way, of feeling embarrassed that he'd interrupted, but also having a clear understanding that his Poppa was near the end.

And in those seconds he wondered if the old man was thinking that his life had been too much hard work and toil. After all, wasn't that his usual complaint? He expected that his grandfather might say that he'd had a "damned backbreaking life" being a worker, an unforgiving existence, but instead the old man smiled at him and said, "It wasn't enough, you know. I wish I'd had a lot more." And Alex had grunted at him, walking on quickly. He didn't need to ask what his Poppa was referring to. He knew. Life. The old man, in the end, wanted more of it. Not in a greedy way. Not in the harsh, uncompromising, critical way that Alex had come to be so familiar with. The old man saw something beautiful that he'd never noticed before.

It was a comforting memory, one that gave him a glimmer of hope in this darkened cemetery. He turned to Marta, wanting to tell her about it, when he noticed a flashing blue light out of the corner of his eye. They were near the entrance, and a police car was slowly patrolling by, a searchlight shining out its passenger window. Alex ran instantly. Before he even gave himself a chance to think through his options. He hid behind a large gravestone, thinking that Marta would do the same, but she stayed rooted to the spot. The searchlight shone on her, and the car stopped. An older policeman emerged from the passenger side, putting the light down on the seat behind him.

"Is your name Marta?" asked the policeman.

Marta nodded, frozen to the spot.

"I've got a worried dad who's going to be very pleased to see you again," he said.

Alex stared hard at his friend's back. What would she do? Tell them about him? Say he was somewhere in the cemetery? He perched up onto his haunches, ready to run if he had to. Marta looked up at the policeman, then said, "I think I want to go home now."

They walked out of the cemetery and Marta climbed into the car. It paused for a minute or two before driving off. Now Alex ran. He knew that Marta wouldn't be able to lie to the police all evening. She could do it in short bursts, but she didn't have the ability to sustain a lie for a long time. That took practice.

He had to find the Jockey and the old thief. How could he possibly explain that to Marta? He had to find them and do something with this slow, burning certainty that rose inside him. He didn't know what to call it, but he knew there was no way he could ignore it. It had been building for nearly two years, and if there were ancient ancestors watching over him tonight, then they would understand his need to act, to hunt down the terror and end it, one way or another.

CHAPTER TWENTY-FIVE

Time was running out. There was a pale light emerging on the horizon, hidden behind the city buildings. The night sky was giving way to a false dawn, a protracted glow that made anyone watching it impatient for the real show to begin, the sunrise.

Alex had arrived at the dam to see that the surrounding area was completely deserted. No sleeping bodies, no tents or huts or any other sign of dwelling. The woman at the campsite had said that the thief hung out here, which might mean he only showed up during the daytime. Alex couldn't wait that long. The police would be talking to Marta right now, asking her why she ran off, what she was doing. He could see Marta's face. Perhaps her mom or dad was there, or both. They'd tell her she had sinned for running away, for being with that un-Christian boy. How could she argue with that? She'd stolen, lied, made her parents distraught. How much more un-Christian could she get? Yes, eventually it would all come out so that Marta could feel good again, could feel that her parents loved her, and that they wanted her back in the church.

It *had* to come out. And then they'd come looking for him.

An old brick restroom stood among some trees, nestled off the main path. It seemed deserted, although it was probably still in use. Alex went into the men's side to relieve himself, standing up against the urinal, trying to stay awake. Maybe this was it. He'd done all he could. He'd followed the thief's trail to the dam and found nothing. Nobody could ask much more of him than that, could they? But even as he had these thoughts he felt repelled by how pathetic they sounded. Imagine what the Jockey would make of him, the stories that would shoot around the school. "Hey, did you hear about the Grub? Thought he'd killed some guy. Nearly wet himself . . ." Alex sighed, closing his eyes, swaying slightly back and forth. What was he doing here? What was he?

What?

He sensed the danger before he heard it. Then the noise registered, a slight scrape, rubber on concrete, a leaf pushed by a shoe, a footfall.

Someone was in the bathroom with him. He didn't turn, not right away. Damned if he'd give them that pleasure. He zipped himself, then casually stepped away from the urinal, pretending he didn't have a care in the world. Only the tension in his body betrayed what was really going on. His mind calculated possibilities. Run into a stall, and then be trapped. Push past, and get nabbed. Stay and fight, use surprise, swing a punch or two.

He turned slowly.

"Little Alex," said the Jockey, a superior grin on his face.

"Little Jockey," he replied, smiling back.

"Haven't gone to bed yet?" The Jockey smirked.

Alex ran at him, swinging a wild punch that the Jockey easily blocked before stepping inside and attempting to grab Alex's arms, to pin him down. Alex was able to slip away, twisting around to kick him hard in the shin.

"Whoa!" yelled the Jockey, sidestepping, then taking Alex by his jacket collar. He used his sheer strength to push him down, drive Alex's body to the concrete floor of the bathroom. Then he pushed his knees into Alex's back. "You finished?" said the Jockey in his ear.

"No," said Alex, his face squeezed into the concrete floor.

"Whatya want, Alex?" said the Jockey, a hint of concern in his voice. "Eh? Whatya after? To get back at me? To get revenge? That's a bit frigging funny, don't you think?" The Jockey eased his pressure. "After all, it was you and your old man who done me in. You were the only one I wasn't careful with. So get over it."

He stepped off Alex's back. Alex got slowly up onto his knees, rubbing the skin on his cheeks, brushing himself down. This was so familiar, on the bathroom floor, humiliated.

"I was just a kid back then!" shouted Alex, getting up onto his feet. "I didn't know that you were for real. I thought you were just making up stories." Tears flowed down his cheeks, and he tried to stem them, tried to smash them away with the back of his hands, but they would not be held back.

"Take it easy, little bro," said the Jockey, his face softening.

For the briefest of moments, they looked each other in the eye, and the bond between them held them to the spot. Big brother and little brother, older and younger, two shavings from the same block of wood.

"Come on," said the Jockey. "You're alive. No one really hurt ya. Besides, I didn't do this weekend thing to get back at ya . . . Well, not completely, anyway."

This was what Alex had come for, and he took a step forward, about to ask what had really been going on, when a hard voice spoke behind him.

"What the hell is he doing here?"

It was the old man, the thief, the Jockey's partner. Alex turned to see him in the doorway. He had a raw, red mark on his face, obviously a trophy from the fall. Other than that, he seemed to be untouched.

"Little punk," said the old man, taking a menacing step toward him.

Alex moved back, almost tripping on the Jockey, who grabbed his arms, saying, "Easy, little guy. Don't get excited . . ."

"I owe you something," said the old man.

"Na, leave him," said the Jockey, releasing his grip on Alex. "He might still . . . you know . . ."

Alex turned to the Jockey. There it was again, a secret purpose, the same secret he'd seen in the old man's laughs, his sneers, his shared grins with the Jockey.

"Oh yes," said the man, regarding Alex in a calculating manner. "He could still be useful, I suppose. As long as he doesn't try to kill me again."

He burst into laughter, nasty and humiliating, the kind of finger-pointing, circling laughter that Alex knew only too well. It filled the bathroom and transformed the Jockey's smile into something hard and provoking.

Alex winced, ashamed of how easily he'd been sucked in. "What is going on?" he said. "What the hell do you want me to do?"

"Now, now," said the old man, poking Alex painfully in the chest. "Don't get too far ahead of yerself. Still gotta prove your worth . . ."

"He found us here, didn't he?" said the Jockey.

"Yep, I suppose you've got a point there. . . ."

They began discussing Alex as if he were a used car, sizing up his strengths and weaknesses, going over his achievements. Every now and then the old man would give Alex a calculating look.

"Persistent little bugger, ain't ya?" he said. "Maybe you've got some hidden talents? You're little, that's good. Scrawny, even, but you punch like a girl . . ."

"Oh yeah?" shouted Alex. "Didn't stop you from crying like a girl up on the bridge when I hit ya."

The man smiled, enjoying Alex's defiance. "He's a bit of a fighter, eh?" he said to the Jockey. "Maybe you two should have a bit of a go, then. See how tough he really can be."

"Yeah?" said the Jockey. "You reckon?"

"Yep," said the thief. "Test him out a bit." He turned to Alex. "Go on, kid. Take him on, see what you're made of."

"No way," said Alex. "I'm going."

How dare they just talk about him as if he was a prospect. He'd come here expecting to end the bond between himself and the Jockey, and they were just making a mockery of it all. Everything about the night had been a total lie. The Jockey wasn't interested in making him a man. He wasn't interested in anything other than his own stupid revenge.

Alex could feel this depressing fact bringing him down, grinding him back into the cold, hard reality of who he really was. But another voice spoke, urged him to stay tall. He'd done stuff that night—acted, thought, protected, been brave—the Jockey had even helped him do some of it. How could he go back to being that stupid kid who taunted the seniors to feel alive?

Take it up with the Jockey, demanded the voice. *Get an answer.*

So Alex marched up to his guide, his mentor, and pushed him

hard in the chest. "You're a total prick, you know that? You said I was your little brother. You taught me stuff, and now you say it's all bull." He pushed him again and again.

"Yeah," said the man, clapping his hands. "That's the way. Swing a punch."

The words snapped in Alex's brain, and he pulled his arm back and swung violently, but once again he was easily blocked.

"Not like that," said the Jockey.

Alex swung again and was again blocked.

"Hey!" shouted the Jockey. "Look at me. You're all wrong."

Alex stopped, staring, panting.

"You're, like, letting the whole frigging world know you're about to hit me. Why don't you put a frigging flashing sign on your head while you're at it. This is girly fighting, Alex, you can do better than that. Where do you reckon a real punch starts, eh?"

"What?" said Alex, confused by this lesson in the middle of his rage.

"Where does a punch begin? How do you start one?"

"I don't know," he said. "You swing your arm . . ."

"Wrong," said the Jockey. "It starts in your shoulder. Look at ya. You got your shoulder leading away from the punch, no power in that. And you got your hand swinging way back to pick up momentum, but it's just saying, 'Here I come! Watch out!' Swing from your shoulder, Alex. Put that into it. Try again."

They were back again, teacher and student, learning the necessary things about life.

"Come on," said the man. "Stop slapping him like a kitten. Show him what you've got."

Alex threw a sharp right cross at the Jockey, exploding from the shoulder, heaving his weight into it. The blow glanced the Jockey on the chin, and he clapped his hands.

"That's more like it," he said, putting a patronizing arm around Alex's shoulder.

"He's got potential, eh?" said the man.

"I told ya that, didn't I?"

"He sure is little, reminds me of you . . ."

"He's got plenty of guts . . ."

"I suppose he'll get better at looking after himself . . ."

Alex listened from some far-off place, the Jockey's arm still on his shoulder, the older man and the older boy, a small fraternity. Their secret started to slowly take shape, one that involved stolen goods and night work. He studied the man's face, looked at his features, and the truth slammed home like a fist to the stomach. They were related.

"Is this, like, your old man?" said Alex.

They stopped their running assessment and looked at him.

"I told ya, I never saw my dad again," said the Jockey. Then he turned to the old man and smiled. "But this here is my uncle. Taught me everything I know. Who do ya think I was with the night they arrested me? You don't reckon I done that job alone, do ya?"

The man nodded his head. "That was gonna be a good job, I tell ya. We were in and doing fine until the coppers turned up. And all because of your daddy." He smiled wickedly at Alex.

So it wasn't him they were after, it was his father. Yet he was somehow involved. He listened to them, still going over some kind of scheme that seemed very important to them. Talking over plans and possibilities, mentioning Alex every now and then, not by name, but by his new moniker, "The Kid." They were going to rob a shop. An electrical shop.

He froze.

Revenge.

Of course, he'd been tested that night for one reason. To join this crew and rob his own father's store. To drive the knife twice into his father's heart. Robbed by his own son. It was a plan that was as sick as it was bold. The whole night had been one long recruitment drive. That was all.

He felt a sudden nausea in his stomach. A revulsion at the lives of these two, living out their sordid, miserable existence, stealing from ordinary people like his dad, using and abusing and hating everything else. The whole world was an opportunity for them to scheme, to plot, to hurt whoever got in their way. And now they were casually discussing making him one of them, until it suited them to dump him.

He could feel the Jockey's arm on his shoulder, a slimy deadness, a weight that didn't belong there.

When you do something, you make sure it hurts for keeps.

He could feel the man's breath on his face, hot, sour, repulsive.

When you say something, you make sure it cuts.

He rejected them. They had no respect for him, no regard at all. He rejected them, because for the first time in years, he respected himself. Without another thought for what he was doing there or how he'd arrived, Alex threw a punch that came from pure shoulder, pure rage, and took the Jockey completely by surprise.

An act of survival.

Then he ran.

CHAPTER TWENTY-SIX

He managed to get around to the back of the bathroom before they could gather themselves and chase him. His punch had bought him very little time. The area around the dam was mostly flat grassy hills, with the trees behind the block offering the only hiding spots. The dawn was truly on its way now, and a gray light showed up gaps in the trees, revealing spaces and clearings, wiping out any hope of concealment with each passing minute.

He had a second, maybe two, to make a decision, and instantly scrambled up the drainpipe of the bathroom, pulling his weight with his skinny arms, ignoring the pain in his knuckles from the punch. He heaved himself up onto the roof, then heard the Jockey's voice from below.

"Will you just stop running and listen?" said the Jockey.

He sounded so reasonable.

Alex stood on the old tin roof of the bathroom, then ran to

the other edge, leaping over piles of rubble and bricks that had either been thrown up there or dumped years ago. The Jockey's uncle was watching him on the other side, hands on hips, making sure Alex knew there'd be no escape this way.

"Alex," said the Jockey. He was on the roof, now. A tiny trickle of blood flowed from his lip. "Why'd you come back?"

Alex met him, face-to-face, eye to eye. A wind blew across his hair, brushing it aside. A sound rattled in the bushes below them. A bird started her morning song. He was the hunter. He did not move. He was as still as the earth. He could hear a faraway voice, *"What is the one creature that will defeat a lion?"* He held the Jockey in an unshakable gaze.

"I came back to finish this," he said, answering the question.

"Yes," said the Jockey, licking at the blood. "I know what you mean. But you don't have to do that. Listen, there's stuff going on here. Me and my uncle, we've got a real business happening. I mean, we're making serious money. No bull. We could use you. Look at ya, you're still little. You're about as big as I was a few years back. You can get into places that I can't no more."

"The lion is cunning, but you must stay true to yourself." Alex closed his eyes, saw the red glow through his eyelids, heard his own heart beating. He opened his eyes again and turned, looking back down at the ground where the Jockey's uncle stood.

"You listen to him, son," shouted the old man. "You could earn some real money. Buy yourself a mobile phone, stereo, DVD player. You'll be respected."

If he jumped, would he land okay or hurt his ankles? Would he have time to recover and run before the man got to him?

"Believe me, I'm better at this now," said the Jockey.

"The lion will purr like a kitten, then strike like a demon." Alex turned back to the Jockey. The roof was too narrow to try to run

past him. He took all these details in calmly, calculating every step, every move, every possible option. He flexed his muscles, bent his knees, then spoke, stalling for time. "You want me to crawl through windows for you?"

"Yeah, that's all. You saw all them boxes of things up on the bridge. That was our warehouse. We'll be needing a new one now, but that's cool. The place was a frigging pain, getting all that stuff up and down that ladder. . . ."

How easily he included him now, made him one of the team, a valuable member of the fraternity. *"The lion will even flatter you to get to your soft underbelly."* Alex felt like spitting at the Jockey for bringing him in to the inner circle, for revealing details he wouldn't dream of telling anyone else. They'd be slashed to ribbons for even knowing it. But he told *him*. Alex. Their little scrambler for tricky little windows.

"You want me to rob my own dad's store?"

"He's got insurance," said the Jockey.

"He's my father . . ."

"What do you care about him? He does nothing but give you grief. He hassles you, yells at ya, calls you useless names . . ."

Alex looked over at the dawn, the sun poking above the trees now, squirting golden light at them. It sparkled off buildings, cutting thin knives across the dewy grass. He thought of the campers in the cemetery, their fire would be burned low by now. When they woke they'd tend to it, stoke it up, make breakfast, then maybe go to those jobs they talked about. He thought about the singers in the park, each home now, guitars safely stored away. He thought about the other "uncle," the way the old man had looked at Max with so much pride and hope rolled into one, the way he'd included Alex in the tribe of men.

"I have real respect," said Alex quietly.

"Yeah? So what?" said the Jockey. "I know that . . ."

"No, you don't know," he said.

"What's respect got to do with anything?" said the Jockey.

And Alex smiled. Slowly, unnerving, calm and sure. He could stand eye to eye with death, he could roar so loud it would bring the trees down, he could run so fast that none would catch him, and he could strike with deadly accuracy.

"My father is a good man," he said, savoring every word. "And there is no way in frigging, freezing hell that I would help you, or your stinking uncle, to rob him or anyone else."

The Jockey's face hardened. He bent casually, picked up half a brick and said, "You mean it?"

He didn't wave the brick menacingly, didn't hover it in the air, but Alex knew perfectly well what his intentions were. Say "Yes" and he was a threat to them. Back off and he'd avoid the pain. But then what would his life be? A life of waiting, of watching? Of looking over his shoulder for the Jockey's next act of revenge?

Say what you mean. Mean what you do. You bet he meant it.

"Yes," said Alex. "I'm not gonna do what you want me to do."

The Jockey's reaction was swift. Alex dodged as soon as he saw the throw, but once again he hadn't counted on the Jockey's cunning. Instead of the brick aiming for his head, it smashed into his foot, breaking his big toe with a crack. Alex crumpled to the roof, crying out in pain.

"What are you doing to him up there?" shouted the Jockey's uncle.

"Teaching him a lesson," said the Jockey, standing over Alex. He prodded him in the stomach with his foot. "What did you think I was gonna do? Let you wander off? Forget about what you saw? What I just told you? You little snot-face. I trusted you.

I thought you'd want to come in on it all. Jeezus, Alex. You've really disappointed me."

He pushed him harder with his foot and Alex rolled over, clutching his shoe, the numb pain in his toe taking his breath away. He looked out across the clearing and saw a car rolling gently down the path toward them. It didn't have its lights flashing. It didn't sound its siren. Perhaps they wanted to surprise them. Alex wasn't about to spoil the party, but the Jockey had other ideas.

"Cops!" he yelled.

His uncle reacted instantly, running into the trees, leaving his nephew to it. The Jockey turned to join him.

Alex rolled over.

It happened in a brief second.

How could he let his teacher go? The Jockey would hurt other people. He'd rob, he'd take, he'd smash. His father would understand. Sometimes you just have to act, even when there's no time to imagine all the possible outcomes.

Alex reached out with his hand and grabbed the Jockey's ankle.

And felt so tall in that moment, so proud of himself. Then he pulled on the departing Jockey's leg with all his strength, bringing him down.

He enjoyed the thud as the boy landed on the roof face-first. But the fighter in the Jockey never stayed down for too long. He was up onto his knees in seconds, advancing. No lessons this time. No big brother and little brother. The Jockey's intention was perfectly clear. His hard, uncompromising hand pushed once.

"Stop it, I'll fall . . ."

Pushed again as the police car came to a halt.

"Stop . . ."

Pushed for the third time as a young officer ran around to the back of the bathroom and the older policeman stood at the front. Pushed so hard, so cruelly, separating Alex from the cradle of the roof, presenting him to the law of gravity, that judged him, that sentenced him to the hard ground.

He fell. His soft head cracking on the concrete below. Shutting down all around him.

As he lay there, unconscious, he didn't see the other car pull up, his friend running to him with a grave look of fear and sadness in her face. Didn't know that she knelt over him, crying, "Alex! Alex!"

Didn't witness the ambulance come, or the arrival of his father, who sat with him as they raced to the hospital, holding his hand. Who spoke to him.

"Stay with me, son. Stay with me."

Because if he'd been able to hear, he would have answered his father, would have spoken the words of courage, would have given him his bond.

"I will."

CHAPTER TWENTY-SEVEN

What a dream he was having. Running. Strong, free, running across the savanna, his legs pumping, his heart racing, his eyes clear and wide, searching for prey. Bearing down on the soft brown hide of a young buck, waiting for that perfect moment when the rhythm of his gait matched the roll of the ground beneath him. When he could push with his powerful back legs and strike.

This was what he lived for. That perfect moment where life met death. Where the hunter and the hunted were joined together in an intimacy that none other could share. It was cruel beauty, harsh poetry, violent harmony. He was united with all things: the wind that rushed through his fur, the scent that filled his nostrils, the very cracks in the earth that the pads of his paws negotiated. He was at one with all living creatures; free to roam, to run, to express the pure power that lay in his every sinew.

And then he had to wake.

It took many attempts before he could make sense of what his eyes revealed to him. Where was the tall grass? The birds flying overhead? And what were these sounds? No distant calls. No wind swish-swishing through the leaves. No deep booming of hooves on the ground.

Voices.

He heard them everywhere. Strange words were hurled at him.

A name.

Alex.

Could he be that entity?

Alex.

He closed his eyes, tried to bring the plains back again, but they were shadowy now, wavering in and out of his vision.

He woke again. A concerned face. A hand touch.

Then more sleep.

The next time he woke he stared at the hospital room a full five minutes before speaking.

"I'm thirsty," he said.

And his father and mother came rushing to the bed, crying, saying, "Oh, Alex. Alex. You're back."

"Yes," he croaked. "I'm Alex."

Marta came to visit him later. She sat on the edge of his bed glancing nervously out the small window from his room to the corridor. Alex followed her gaze and saw Mrs. Zubrinowicz patrolling, nodding to him in a half friendly, half hostile way.

"She's keeping an eye on me," said Marta apologetically.

"Oh," said Alex. Then, "Why?"

"Apparently you're a bad influence on me," said Marta, allowing herself to smile. "I told Mom that it was a Christian thing to do. . . . You know . . . come to help you that Friday night. Even if it did mean I had to take Dad's mobile phone . . . and borrow some cash. She used to think you were un-Christian. Now she says you've, you know, corrupted me or something."

Alex smiled, closing his eyes. "Like a computer, eh?"

"Yes," said Marta. "You're a virus. Wait until she hears about what happened today."

Alex opened his eyes, alert now. "Okay," he said. "What *did* happen?"

Marta could barely contain herself. "It was at school. The seniors, you know, were just being themselves, I guess. Kicking a soccer ball around. They weren't bothering me, or calling me names like they usually do. But they were laughing. I don't know . . . There was something about them all laughing together, as if life was so cool for them. As if *they* could be happy, and everyone else . . ."

She paused, and he leaned over to his side table to get a drink but felt dizzy. Marta helped him sit up, then retrieved the glass of water for him. Alex took a sip or two, then asked, "What did you do?"

She smiled. "I took their soccer ball away."

"Really?"

"Yep. Just grabbed it. They went crazy, called me horrible names, but I wouldn't give it back. Barry Pilsener said they should dunk me."

Now Alex laughed, but it hurt his head so he had to close his eyes for a moment to allow the thumping in his brain to subside.

"Anyway, a teacher came and tried to sort things out. Said I should give the ball back. And I guess I should have, but it was like he was a part of the laughing and the seniors and all that. So I said to him, 'This is not a happy school.' He wasn't that interested. Nobody was. They just wanted everything to return to the way it had always been. In the end, I threw their silly ball in the air, then kicked it as hard as I could."

"Wow," said Alex. "That's, like, ten years of sinning all bound up in one for you."

"It gets worse," said Marta, a mischievous gleam in her eye.

"This I wanna hear . . ."

"The ball smashed a window."

"Oh, man!" said Alex, laughing so much that it took almost five minutes for his head *and* toe to stop hurting. Once he had calmed down and taken another drink of water, he turned to his friend and said, "I'm glad you're corrupted."

"Me, too," said Marta.

She held his hand, angling her body so that her mother could not see their touch. They didn't speak for a while, mainly because Alex had drifted off into a sleep. Eventually he opened his eyes, staring into the distance, a far-off look in his eyes.

"I've been remembering stuff," he said. "Half the time I don't know if it's a dream or it really happened, but I remember."

"It's all true," whispered Marta. "The Jockey is in jail again. He tried to worm his way out of it all with lies, but no one believed him." She stopped, held Alex's gaze, then added, "You were so brave."

He closed his eyes and smiled, feeling that calm, assured peace inside him. A cool breeze blew into the room, wafted against his skin, bringing scents and sounds from far-off places. It was so beautiful, spoke of wind-song, birdsong, rustling leaves. Minted grass and fragrant flowers. When he opened his eyes again, he was surprised to see Marta sitting by his bed.

"How long have you been here?" he asked.

"I've . . . I came . . . before. Remember?"

He nodded. Yes, he could see that might have happened. All things were blending into one another at the moment, revealing how connected they were, how integral to each other every living thing was.

It was a beautiful show.

He watched a tear come to Marta's eye, and somehow it blended into a packet of chocolate biscuits in her hand. Now he reveled in the smile on her face, and he smiled, too, remembering again their afternoons. It was like finding an old toy that you'd almost forgotten about.

He tried to eat one, but it was too sweet, too rich, so instead he enjoyed Marta eating too many too quickly, smiling as she sat back with satisfaction. Marta looked at him and said she'd just remembered a tiny little detail of her long afternoon after the broken window.

"I was sitting in that room outside the principal's office," she said.

"Yeah, I know it," said Alex grimly.

"And the Bald Eagle walked by, and he hadn't been involved or anything, but I could tell he was angry. And he looked at me and said, 'Happy now?'"

"What did you say?" asked Alex. "Did you say, 'Yes'?"

Marta leaned over his bed and took his hand. "I did," she said.

And they laughed.

The packet of chocolate biscuits slid off the bed between them and landed on the floor. None fell out, none broke. They were unspoiled and perfect in every way. A miracle, which they didn't even see.